DATE DUE

The Moon's Fireflies

Stories by

Benjamin Madison

OOLICHAN BOOKS
FERNIE, BRITISH COLUMBIA, CANADA
2010

Copyright © 2010 by Benjamin Madison ALL RIGHTS RESERVED. No part of this publication may be reproduced, stored in a retrieval system, or transmitted, in any form or by any means, without prior written permission of the publisher, except by a reviewer who may quote brief passages in a review to be printed in a newspaper or magazine or broadcast on radio or television; or, in the case of photocopying or other reprographic copying, a licence from ACCESS COPYRIGHT, 6 Adelaide Street East, Suite 900, Toronto, Ontario M5C 1H6.

Library and Archives Canada Cataloguing in Publication

Madison, Benjamin, -
    The moon's fireflies / Benjamin Madison.

Short stories.
ISBN 978-0-88982-263-4

    I. Title.

PS8626.A33M66 2010   C813'.6   C2010-901620-3

All persons and places in these stories are products of the author's imagination and any similarity to actual people or places is purely coincidental.

We gratefully acknowledge the financial support of the Canada Council for the Arts, the British Columbia Arts Council through the BC Ministry of Tourism, Culture, and the Arts, and the Government of Canada through the Book Publishing Industry Development Program, for our publishing activities.

Cover illustration by Corinna Zimmermann

Published by
Oolichan Books
P.O. Box 2278
Fernie, British Columbia
Canada V0B 1M0

www.oolichan.com

Printed in Canada

Text printed on 100% post consumer recycled FSC-certified paper.

Mixed Sources
Product group from well-managed forests,
controlled sources and recycled wood or fiber
www.fsc.org   Cert no. SW-COC-003438
©1996 Forest Stewardship Council

With respect and affection, these stories are dedicated to the people of West Africa and to their children.

TABLE OF CONTENTS

I

Odi Sah! / 11
Junior's Store / 21
Clifford / 33
Nothing Happens / 43
Greetings / 49
Affiong / 59
Night Studies / 67
Mamy Wata / 75
That Cassius / 83
Big Snake Coming! / 89
One of the Boys from Home / 95
Ekpo I / 103
Ekpo II / 110
Expo / 121
Season of the Tsum / 131
The Bridge I / 141
The Bridge II / 155
Anniversary / 165

II

Cowardly Baboons / 175
Unique Data / 181

Afterword / 193

I

Odi Sah!

The canoe is about seven meters long and a meter and a half wide. It is crowded with a dozen women and their children. Most of the women have a placid baby strapped to their backs and a toddler leaning against them. They all have large cloth-wrapped bundles bulging with mysterious lumps. The women wear wax print wrappers with the bold designs and bright colors favored here. They talk and laugh with the ease and familiarity of old friends. As we slide over the brown waters of the Cross River a light breeze rises and lifts the oppressive heat. I trail my hand in the water—it is just exactly body temperature, like the air. The canoe touches the shore from time to time as the small outboard carries us downstream. At each place a few women disembark and others enter, settling themselves, their bundles and their children, while chatting and laughing. The river and the mangroves meet in a tangle of roots and mud, the land along the edge of the river being barely above water level. Villages are set back above the beaches, invisible in the rainforests on higher ground.

I am making a first visit to a friend in Effiat Mbo, a large village located near the mouth of the Cross River in Southeastern Nigeria. After one stop, the *etiubo* (father of the canoe) calls to me in broken English to inquire where I am going. From our communication, largely in gestures, I am made to understand that the canoe stopped at Effiat Mbo some time ago and he is now on his way further south. He is surprised I did not know the place where I wanted to disembark. I had assumed he would inform me of this. After a few moments of thought he suggests I get out of the canoe and wait on the shore until he returns on his homeward voyage. He will drop me at Effiat Mbo on the way back. Although I feel some reluctance, I agree and he points the canoe towards the shore.

A few minutes later I am alone on a small patch of sandy beach between longer stretches of mud and mangrove. There are no visible signs of human life. Aside from crocodiles and snakes there are no dangerous animals in this part of Africa but it is a little eerie to be alone so far from all I have ever known. There are no crocodiles or snakes visible nearby so I sit down on a log and try to relax to the lazy hum of the insects and the tranquil calls of the birds. But there seems something sinister in the surrounding forest. I begin to imagine painted warriors lurking behind the trees. Are those birdcalls I hear genuine? I stand up and look around. Everything seems peaceful. Perhaps the canoe-driver has some kind of arrangement with people around here that he will drop unsuspecting passengers like myself on this deserted bit of shoreline. I hear a sudden sound behind me and spin around.

There is a small naked boy standing in front of me, his eyes wide with excitement.

"*Odi* sah!" (Welcome sir!) bursts out of him, accompanied by an excited smile. He looks harmless, certainly no concealed weapons there. I kneel down and smile back in what I hope is a friendly fashion and he launches a series of questions I don't understand. When I am unable to answer, he pats me on the shoulder to indicate I am not to go away and races off into the forest.

Ten minutes later he returns at full speed with three other small boys dressed like himself and a larger boy wearing shorts. This boy has been to school and can speak some English.

"Please sah, my father says you will come and kiss his house."

I look up into the dark forest and briefly consider the range of dismemberment rituals likely available there. The beach suddenly seems open and safe when compared to the somber, brooding forest. I explain that I must wait on the shore until the canoe returns so that I can continue my journey.

"That is no problem, sir. These small boys can stay here and when they see the canoe they can run and tell us."

Outmaneuvered, I follow him up into the forest. As we enter the darkness beneath the trees, I cast a last glance back and see the small boys, apparently playing on the beach. Everything seems all right but I don't know where we're going or how long it is going to take to get there. I curse myself for being so easily swayed. I should have insisted on remaining on the beach.

As we move through the shadows a small lizard on a tree trunk catches my eye. Its belly is a shining lime green and its back seems to be covered with gold. I've never seen anything like it. When I point it out to the boy he looks at it appreciatively for a moment, then tells me the local name and adds, "We like him," before beckoning me to continue. Occasional rays of sun pierce the green shade and spotlight a leaf, a branch, a black and umber butterfly. A huge tree has fallen across the path and torn a hole in the canopy. Thick shafts of brilliant sunlight pour through the gaps and make the mossy log glow. The boy leaps nimbly into the light and turns round.

"Please, Sah. Give me your bag." I hand him the pack. Then he extends his hand to help me climb over the log. But my slippery soles do not provide the same purchase as his sure bare feet and slide out from under me when I am halfway over. I tumble backwards onto the soft pathway. He falls beside me but is up on one elbow in an instant brushing moss off my shoulders.

I am completely unhurt, just stunned, and as I look up into his worried face I am struck by the beauty of African children. It's not simply perfect symmetry of feature. Innocence and tranquil joy shine there, the true light of childhood. This boy looks like he also enjoys good humor. An impish grin lurks at the edges of his concerned expression. I remember, there is a time when falling down is funny.

"Why are you laughing, Sah?"

"Sometimes, we need to fall down." I sit up and we continue to shake the dirt and leaves from my shirt. "And why are you laughing?"

"Because your hat is not correct." He straightens my cap to his satisfaction. "There!"

Although I have been in Africa for almost a month now, I continue to arrive anew almost every day. With each arrival a little more of me is here, but a little more of me is left behind as well. When I am fully here, I will not be the same person who departed on this journey.

"Sah, what is your name?"

For just one blinding second, I do not know the

answer to this question. Then I recall myself and tell him. He is called Akpan. We mount the log again, successfully this time, and shortly afterwards we arrive at his father's compound, a large mud house built of the red earth found here and roofed with intricately woven palm thatch turned bronze by the sun.

The father comes out of the house and gives me his ten—this is the full handshake of honor, given with both hands clasped over those of the visitor. Children rush from all directions, tumbling out of the doors and windows of the houses and calling, "*Mbatang! Odi!*" I am soon seated in the parlor. The rust-colored earthen floor of the house is smooth and has been immaculately swept. About fifteen women and children peek through the doorway at me, too shy to come in. The father seats himself beside me and, with the assistance of his son's translation, discovers my reason for being on their beach, then inquires where I am from. I explain that I have come to Nigeria from America to teach in Udong Community School in the village of Akai Isong. My answer makes him happy. He is related to Junior, the man who runs the Akai Isong village store that I often visit. But now that I am here in their village, he suggests, why don't I stay with them? I explain why I must return to Akai Isong. This plunges the father into gloom.

"My father wishes you to stay here very much," says the boy.

There is some discussion between father and son and then I am asked, "Sah! How do you like your beer—warm or hot?" There is no electricity in these villages so bottled drinks are either at air temperature (hot) or have been slightly cooled by sitting in a large clay pot full of water (warm). A few minutes later a table is placed before me, bearing a liter bottle of Star Beer (warm) and a glass. At a signal from his father the boy deftly uncaps the bottle with his teeth and pours the beer. While I sip the beer, Akpan and his father hold a lengthy discussion.

"Since you are not going to stay with us, Sah, my father wishes to ask you a favor," says Akpan.

"What can I do?"

"Sah, my father says he wishes to give me to you."

"I'm sorry, I don't understand."

"You will take me as your child, Sah." Akpan appears comfortable with this idea and smiles shyly at me as he makes the proposal.

I stumble and stutter over a reply but Akpan is ahead of me. "I can help you in your house in Akai Isong and go to school there."

I look up at the thatch overhead. How can I tell this child that I don't want him?

"I'm sorry. I can't. It's not allowed. My contract, the papers say, 'No children.'"

"Sah?"

"Government contract, government says I cannot have children," I lie desperately. Father and son are sinking into depression. I ask Akpan about the school he has attended in the past. He explains that his father was able to send him to another village for schooling for three years. For the last year there has been no money for school fees and he has remained at home. I sip a little of the beer and propose a solution to the father.

"Look, you're related to Junior. How about if Akpan goes to stay with Junior in Akai Isong? I will be happy to pay his school fees and buy his uniform and books."

The boy's face lights with a smile and he eagerly translates my suggestion for his father. Fees for primary school here are only about twenty dollars per year, but this is often an insurmountable barrier for poor Nigerian families.

"And you can help Junior with his store, since his own children are still too small," I add, developing this idea, and hoping that Junior will accept it.

Akpan's father is beginning to look more hopeful and discusses the possibility with Akpan. Then Akpan goes out and returns again with a woman I suspect is his mother. There is more discussion. Akpan is unable to stay still and keeps jumping up and going from one parent to the other.

"Sah, my mother says you are very kind. But she asks if I cannot stay with you."

"Oh, I'm afraid not. It's not possible."

"She says if I stay with you I will become very smart."

"You can come and visit me and help to keep my compound clean."

"Oh, thank you, Sah!" He translates my suggestion to his mother, who seems to feel that even this much exposure to me will result in a little transfer of smartness.

Soon it is settled. When I return to Akai Isong from Effiat Mbo I will go to Junior and put the idea to him. If he agrees, we will send word by the canoe-driver.

Calls of "*Mbatang!*" still echo in the village outside and as I sip the beer, I think about this greeting to white people, always shouted with the utmost friendliness. *Mbatang* literally means, "Those who carry us away." It is a relic of the slave trade. Enveloped in such genuine hospitality and trust, I can only marvel at the savagery of those first Europeans visiting these shores.

Some time after I finish drinking the beer, Akpan steps in to say that the message chain of small boys has reported the imminent arrival of the canoe. To show me how he will look in his school uniform he is now dressed in a dazzling white shirt and blue shorts. He insists on carrying my pack. His father and mother and about twenty children accompany us down to the beach, where the canoe is idling in the shallows. I give the father my ten and step into the canoe. Akpan has already stowed my pack. His father exchanges a few words with the *etiubo*. The family stands on the shore and waves as we move up the river.

Junior's Store

Akai Isong is the most central of the seven villages that make up the Udong community. The villages, each consisting of forty or fifty thatched, mud-brick compounds, are all within walking distance, separated by stretches of lush rain forest and small farm clearings. We are within a kilometer of the Cross River and about forty kilometers from the town of Oron in southeastern Nigeria. Junior's store is located where the trail from the school compound intersects the main pathway through the village.

The store is little more than a large window that

opens from a back room of his house onto the path. He has built a few shelves inside the room and a counter on the windowsill. The shelves contain boxes of powdered soap, tins of sardines and condensed milk, sugar cubes, tiny tins of tomato paste, cigarettes (generally sold by the stick), captain's biscuits, instant coffee and tea bags, matches and mosquito coils. Below the counter are cases of beer and soft drinks. Junior also has bread and eggs when a trader in these items has passed through the village.

It is a humble establishment to bear the name of store—most American kitchen cupboards are stocked with a far greater variety and quantity of goods. But people here don't use much that is manufactured or processed in other places, nor do they have the money to buy such things.

The thatch from Junior's roof extends to cover a seating area where two wooden benches face each other, their ends snugged against the wall on either side of the window. When business is quiet these are occupied by children taking advantage of the shade by day or, at night, the yellow glow of the kerosene lantern on the windowsill.

Tonight when I approach the store I can see by the lantern light that there are at least six small children on one of the benches. I return their greetings and sit on the opposite bench. They are giggling and talking quietly and I notice something I often observe here. Though there is room on the bench for them to spread out comfortably, they are all bunched up and tangled together at one end, arms and hands on each other's shoulders and knees. As they move and re-arrange themselves it is difficult to tell where one child stops and the next begins. Every one of them must be in physical contact at a dozen points with the others. I analyze little John, who is about eight years old. His right ankle is crossed over another boy's ankle and bounces up and down in emphasis of what he is saying. Both of his arms curve round the shoulders of the boys next to him and his right hand extends beyond the nearest shoulder to rest on the neck of the next boy on the bench. The rest of them are similarly entangled. Should another child come by he will squeeze himself into this mass quite unnoticeably.

Junior's smiling face appears at the window and we exchange greetings. I ask him to bring me one beer, one for himself and one soft drink. Junior is about thirty. He learned to speak English well in middle school but the expense of going to the city for high school was more than his parents could afford. For this reason he was one of our school's founders, so determined was he that his children would have a high school education available to them in this village. He opens the bottles and places them on the counter. At a word from Junior, John disengages himself from the other children and brings one beer and the soft drink to me. I take a sip of the soft drink and give the bottle to him with a gesture that says it is for all the children.

He says, "Thank you, Sah," and insinuates himself back into the group. They all say "Thank you, Sah" and pass the bottle from hand to hand, each taking a tiny sip as though it were some rare vintage wine.

Junior comes out of his compound gate and sits down with his beer on the bench opposite to me. I am pleased that in this culture I do not need to rush into business but can relax and introduce my topic when the time is right. On my return voyage from Effiat Mbo this morning I realized that I had taken on quite a lot of work by offering to sponsor Akpan in the village school here.

First, of course, I have to broach the subject to Junior, who is key to this plan. I have no idea what his response will be when I suggest he add another child to his household. He has three small children of his own and is busy with his trading, carrying a small stock of his goods to each of the local village markets almost every day. Should he agree to provide Akpan with room and board I still must arrange with the primary school authorities to get him registered properly and ensure that all the papers are in place. Then of course there are his books and other school supplies to be purchased and cloth for his uniforms to be bought and tailored. I have planned to use most of my spare time this week in making sure that all this is done. Tonight is Sunday and I think that by Wednesday I will probably have completed most of these preparations.

After we have gossiped awhile, Junior asks, "How was your trip to Effiat Mbo? Your friend is fine?"

"It was good, thank you," I answer, somewhat surprised that Junior knows where I went. "My friend is fine. I had a good visit."

"But I hear you went a little too far?"

"Yes, I visited another village on the way."

"Akai Ekuyo," says Junior, naming Akpan's village.

"Yes."

"You visited my brother there. How is he?" I have been here long enough to know that Junior is using the word 'brother' in the West African sense that includes any male of the same generation who has any kind of family connection.

"He is fine and sends his greetings to you." Junior seems to be taking the initiative in this conversation but seeing as it is going exactly where I want it to go I have another sip of beer.

"And his family?"

"Fine. He has many children, all very beautiful and healthy."

"Akai Ekuyo is very isolated. If you want to visit you must go by canoe. It is impossible to get in or out even by foot. I have not been down there for a few years. And when I was last there some of his children were away at school."

"Yes, I wanted to talk to you about that."

"I hear you want to sponsor one of them."

"Yes, that's no problem. Your brother's son, Akpan, is a very intelligent boy who should be in school. But he needs a place to stay."

"This Akpan, what is he like? Do you think he is a good boy?"

"He seemed to me to be a very good boy, very smart, very respectful and very sweet. He speaks good English too."

"So you think I should take him into my house?"

"Well, yes, I was hoping."

"And you are going to pay all his school expenses?"

"Yes."

Junior takes a sip of his beer while I sit in suspense.

"I think that will be very nice. My wife will have more time to work on her farms and the boy can help with the children and the store."

Step one completed with amazing ease. Junior must have heard earlier today about my visit to Akpan's village and has had time to decide what to do.

"That's wonderful. This boy will do well in school. He is very intelligent. I'll go to the primary school tomorrow to make the arrangements."

"Why wait until tomorrow? Do you know Ekpenyong? He's the primary school principal."

"No, I haven't met him."

"Then let's go now and settle the business."

We finish our beer and set off down the path to the end of the village where the primary school compound lies.

On the way, Junior tells me that the *etiubo* who took me to Effiat Mbo is his wife's cousin. He told the entire story of my unplanned visit to Akai Ekuyo to his wife who passed it to Junior's wife when they met in the church this afternoon. Junior retells the story as it was told to him, with many pauses for laughter. It seems to be a funny story although the humor of it escapes me.

The primary school principal's house is located near the entrance to the school's compound and Mr. Ekpenyong, the principal, is at home. Soon we are seated in the parlor of his house. On one wall is a large poster of Christ staring morosely upwards while offering a large bleeding heart. This is flanked by two other posters, one depicting a coy young oriental woman dressed in a g-string and bra while seated on the driver's seat of a huge, shiny fork lift. The other poster is a collection of photographs of generals in the Nigerian Army, all looking grim under large military hats generously wreathed with gold braid. Beer is served. In exchange, Junior gives the principal the story of my visit to Akai Ekuyo, which seems to be even funnier in the local language version.

After one particularly hilarious part, the principal turns to me and says, "Please, you must not think we are laughing at you. It is the *etiubo* who is so funny. He knew you wanted to go to Effiat Mbo but was too frightened of you to say anything. Then, after Effiat Mbo was left behind, he began to be frightened that you would be angry that he had not told you. He says he just wanted to jump into the river and leave the canoe to go anywhere it wanted. He was saying in his mind, 'Mama! Mama!, this *mbatang* go kill me!'"

This drives them into peals of laughter.

"Oh," says the principal when he has recovered, "I am very pleased to meet you. Why have you not come to see me before? You must come and look at our school sometime."

"Yes, I would like that. And I want to register a student for your school, do all the paperwork, etcetera."

"Oh, no problem. This boy, Akpan, yes? Junior has given me all the information I need. The boy can start as soon as he gets here."

"That's wonderful!" Step two completed. "I will go to Uduko market tomorrow and buy cloth for his uniform."

"But why go to Uduko? My brother in Akai Efefe has the cloth and is a good tailor." The principal then appeals to Junior to support this idea and rushes out of the room.

"Let us go see his brother," says Junior, "he is a very nice man and a good tailor."

I look at my watch. It is nearly eight o'clock.

"Akai Efefe is not far-far, only about twenty minutes walk from here."

The principal returns, having exchanged his wrapper for a pair of trousers, and we enter the forest on the path to Akai Efefe, a village I have not visited before. The moon is directly overhead and is so bright that its rays pierce the thick foliage high above us and a milky light filters down into the forest. Junior walks in front and flicks his flashlight on and off to ensure we don't step on any snakes or army ant columns.

"You will see many children here," says Junior as we walk. "Too many, I think. Etinwa has twenty-four."

Younger villagers who have had some education, such as Junior, are beginning to see the wisdom of limiting their families. When these villages were first built, there was much land to farm and a greater number of wives and children meant more of it could be farmed. Now the area is circumscribed by other groups and there is no new land for the next generation to exploit. Existing farms, when they are inherited, are becoming smaller and smaller as they are divided between children.

"But, you know, he has so many children only because he is a reasonable man," says the principal, referring to his brother, Etinwa. Then he continues his explanation.

"When Etinwa was first married he wanted to have a son very badly. But his wife bore only daughters, three, I think at first. So he sat down with his wife and they decided that he should take another wife. And this second wife, too, gave birth to daughters, three also. At the same time, the first wife had added another daughter. They all sat down and decided that a third wife was the only answer. So he married again and again only daughters were produced. By this time he had eleven daughters. A fourth wife was added. Meanwhile his second wife gives birth again to another daughter, making twelve daughters in all. Finally, with the fourth wife, a son was born. Etinwa called this first son, 'Thank God.'

"At this time, Etinwa was very happy but he was also troubled. He said, 'What kind family, this? Twelve girls, one boy? This is not correct. It's lop-sided.' So his wives continued to have babies and as though the fourth wife had changed the settings, all were sons. They continued until he had twelve sons to match his twelve daughters. He called the last son, 'My Duty Is Done.' And then he told his wives he didn't want to see them pregnant again."

When we enter Etinwa's compound, I admire his restraint. Children are everywhere and all are beautiful. Some are helping their mothers prepare food and others are playing. The atmosphere is busy and noisy but the business is purposeful and peaceful and the noise is happy. Greetings are called to us from all parts of the compound and smaller children run up to us and take our hands. Etinwa is seated in his parlor reading a newspaper by lantern light and rises to greet us.

Soon beer is brought and the principal and Junior compete in telling the story of my trip to Effiat Mbo. The story seems to get longer and funnier each time it is told. Etinwa has seizures of laughter. I confess the fears I had during this voyage—how I had thought that the canoe-driver had purposely dropped me off where cannibals might catch and eat me. This adds depth to the story and is well received.

In a moment of sobriety, I introduce the topic of uniforms. There will be no problem, I am told. What size is the boy? I begin to make estimates with my hand against the wall.

"Wait! Wait! Wait!" says Etinwa and barks a command out into the compound. Within a few minutes his boys are assembled, all twelve of them, ranging in age from about fourteen to three years. He arranges them in order of size and then directs me to choose the one that is the same size as Akpan. I feel like a visiting general but soon make a selection. The uniform will be delivered tomorrow. Step three completed.

I am not even slightly surprised when another man enters the parlor carrying a selection of exercise books, backpacks, pencils and other student necessities. He is Etinwa's cousin and next-door neighbor and deals in school supplies. But before I can make my selection of supplies he asks a question through Junior.

"He wants to know if he can see your gun."

"My gun? What gun?"

The cousin's explanation in the local language is long and, though it begins seriously, soon degenerates into mirth.

Gasping for breath, Junior explains. "The gun you pointed at the canoe-driver." The cousin has already heard the story of my voyage to Effiat Mbo but in the version he was told, I pull a gun out of my pack and threaten to shoot the *etiubo* when I find that he has not dropped me at the correct place. It takes all my persuasive powers to convince Junior to correct this version of the story. Perhaps I will admit to a knife? I am firm. No weapons.

The school supplies will be delivered tomorrow with the uniforms. We promise to return soon for another visit and say goodnight to Akai Efefe, many of whose residents have gathered at Etinwa's to see the wild white man. It is just ten o'clock. On our way back to Akai Isong, Junior chuckles and says, "We are very pleased to have you with us in our village."

"Thank you. I am very pleased to be here."

"But there is something you can do."

"Yes?"

"We want you to leave us as often as possible. We enjoy your traveling too much!"

Clifford

When we enter the restaurant I greet the young proprietress in the Oron local language. She replies with a sweet smile, then asks us in perfect English what we would like to eat. Oron is a small town located on the Cross River in southeastern Nigeria. The restaurant, with the appealing name, "The Relaxing Depot," is a corrugated iron shack balanced on the edge of the river near the Oron-Calabar Ferry Terminal. When we are seated, Clifford informs me that I am wasting my time learning the Oron language.

"Look," he says, "How many of these people do you

think there are? Maybe fifty thousand, no more. You spend your two years here learning Oron language and what have you got? Nothing. If you go twenty miles in any direction they speak a different language." Clifford pronounces his words precisely and separates them with tiny pauses. He says one must speak like that here or nobody will understand. It has become so habitual with him that even when he is with other native-English speakers he continues to enunciate clearly.

"Well, it's very interesting," I reply weakly. I am thinking about my latest linguistic discovery. Last night while walking along the village path that leads to my house on the school compound, I saw my first fireflies—small greenish lights throbbing on and off in the grass or flickering into brightness like sparks in the velvet night air. I asked the children with me the local name for these wonderful insects.

"*Nta-nta*," they replied. When I later wrote this down in my notebook, I noticed that this word for fireflies is also used in conjunction with *affiang*, the word for moon. *Nta-nta affiang* means 'stars.' The stars are the moon's fireflies.

Clifford doesn't think much of the food when it is served. He is more interested in my shopping list and annotates this carefully, muttering prices to himself while we eat. He says I will be robbed blind if I am not careful. "These people are all thieves," he says. "They've got a different moral code here." His teaching contract is nearly completed but he has decided that one duty he must perform before leaving is to share with a relative newcomer like me the fruit of his years of experience. After lunch I am going for the first time to the large town market to buy some groceries. Convinced that I was being ripped off by the local village market I usually patronize, Clifford has given me a lift into town on his motorcycle and is advising me how to shop.

"Now as soon as they see you coming they have got you marked out—you are a rich white man and that means you are fair game. They are going to ask about ten times the price they would charge a local. Now here is what you do: When you see something you want to buy—say tomatoes—do not look at the tomatoes. Look at something nearby like hot peppers. Pick up a hot pepper and look at it with real disgust. Throw it back on the counter. Pick up another one and ask the price. Just throw it down on the counter when they tell you whatever ridiculous amount they expect you to be sucker enough to pay. They will give you another ridiculous price, but lower. Now at this point it is good to get angry." Clifford mimics anger for me, "What do you think you are doing, trying to charge this much for these rotten peppers? They are not fit for pigs!"

The other patrons of the restaurant, a man and his small son, look over doubtfully. The small boy retreats to safety between his father's knees.

Clifford continues, "Now you have got them

worried. They know you are not some patsy. They will give you another much lower price. Just walk away. They will call out the real price as you walk away. Do not even look back. Just 'notice' the tomatoes and pick one of them up. You might have to do a little performance on the tomatoes too but usually I find that by this time they understand that I am not a sucker. Whatever they ask for the tomatoes, offer them one quarter of the amount. They will come down again."

Clifford goes back to work on my shopping list and I gaze idly out the glassless window to the riverbank below. About a dozen naked children are splashing and playing in the sunlight and their laughter floats up to us like butterflies in a light breeze.

A few minutes later Clifford's voice interrupts my reverie. He is speaking without his usually clipped elocution. "Those kids are really having fun, aren't they?" he muses. "No toys or anything. Poor little buggers."

When I glance at him to answer he is staring out the window like a lost child. Then he grimaces and states with his normal precision, "Probably half of them will be dead this time next year. They might as well be swimming in a toilet." He shakes his head and returns to my shopping list. He is marking next to each item the exact amount I should pay.

The food is delicious and I mention that to the waitress as we leave, just for the pleasure of seeing her smile again. Clifford drops me off at the entrance to the market.

"Look," he says, "just remember that you have to put on a certain face here. You cannot just relax and be yourself or these people will be all over you and before you know it, bingo, you are no better off than they are. It is hard, but it is the only way to survive over here."

The market is a bustling collage of colors and smells and people, and everyone appears to be in a very good mood. Young boys and girls balancing trays of cellophane-wrapped candies on their heads weave between the busy shoppers with the ease and grace of dancers. I find it difficult to keep Clifford's advice in mind. There is much shouting and laughter tossed from stall to stall and mixed with it are so many greetings to me, "*Mbatang!*" that my face aches from smiling in reply.

I squeeze through the press of bodies until I reach the vendors selling food items. There, beneath a patchwork roof of rusty corrugated iron sheets, pieces of cardboard and packing cases, the rickety market stalls are piled with pyramids of brilliant yellow papayas, red and green mangoes, sacks of purple onions and trays of carrots and cucumbers. Long-handled dippers rest in basins of ruby-red palm oil and the humid air is rich with the scents of smoked fish and strange spices. I do want to buy tomatoes and see some that look fresh and ripe. The woman selling them has no peppers for me to finger in disgust so I pick up one of her onions. I realize that I don't know how to look at an onion with disgust. I'll have to practice at home.

The vegetable vendor calls, "Custo-mah!" I look up and she gives me the Oron greeting in a testing tone of voice. I am proud to be able to give her the correct response. She looks at me approvingly and gives me a second, more complicated Oron greeting. Once again I am able to respond correctly. She smiles broadly now and shouts something to the neighboring market women and they all call out their greetings. The tomato seller comes around and pulls me into her stall where she has a small bench. I am seated while she bustles around giving orders to the flock of children who have gathered.

A schoolboy appears with a cold soft drink, uncaps it and pours it for me into a large plastic mug. Clifford's advice has not prepared me for this situation. The schoolboy tells me the tomato seller is his mother and her name is Atim. She would like to ask me some questions. He translates. My grasp of Oron is not adequate for conversation. She is not satisfied until she has me perfectly located and has assured herself that I know several of her relatives in the village where I live and teach. One of her nephews is a student in my English class. Atim nods happily once she has thus established our relationship. When I have finished my drink I look sadly at my watch and explain that I must do some shopping. The son (Tuesday is his name) asks what I want. I mention that I had come to buy tomatoes and his mother has some nice ones. Atim goes to the front of the stall and carefully selects six perfect tomatoes. Then she comes and puts them into my pack. I ask how much they are.

Tuesday says, "They are a gift." When I protest, he adds, "She is giving them to you," as if I am a little dense. Atim is adamant in refusing all payment, extracting only the promise that I will come to see her whenever I am in the town. Her son accompanies me to guide me to what I want to buy and carry my purchases. Sugar is the first item on my list and once again I fail Clifford since, after we exchange greetings with the sugar seller and Tuesday makes introductions, the price I am quoted is lower than the one Clifford has neatly marked on the list. The quoted price is in fact so much lower than Clifford's price that I offer Clifford's price to the shopkeeper, Celestine, in the hope that I can keep everyone happy. "No, no, no," he says, stabbing his finger at Clifford's penciled price, "nobody ever pays so much for sugar." He will accept only the lower price. I cannot bring myself to follow Clifford's injunction to offer less and reach for my wallet to pay for the sugar. My wallet is missing. It's not in any of my pockets or the pack. Has it been stolen? Clifford's sardonic laughter echoes in my mind.

Tuesday and Celestine hold deep discussion. They decide we should return to the last place I remember having my wallet—The Relaxing Depot—and see if anyone along the way has found it. Celestine stuffs the sugar into my pack. He says I can pay for it next time I am in town. He and Tuesday escort me towards the main market entrance. Along the way we are joined by Atim and several of her and the shopkeeper's acquaintances. They develop a plan for searching the street and inquiring from street vendors for the wallet. They all seem to be more concerned than I am and keep patting me on the shoulder to make me feel better. I do a quick calculation. The wallet holds the equivalent of about twenty American dollars.

No sooner do we leave the market, however, than I am hailed, "*Mbatang*!" We stop and a woman comes over to us from where she has been sitting in the deep shade of a mango tree. It is the woman from the restaurant and she holds my wallet in her hand. "You forgot your wallet," she says. She explains that she overheard me say I was going to the market. She knew I would leave by the main entrance and has been waiting here for almost an hour. "You must be more careful," she says and adds, "and you shouldn't carry so much money around like this. There are thieves here." Everyone nods. Celestine, perhaps sensing that I am a little embarrassed by so much solicitude, suggests we all adjourn to his shop for a little refreshment. I thank everyone as well as I am able and explain that I still have to do some shopping.

Atim pretends anger. "Is my son not a schoolboy? Can he not read your shopping list? Why am I paying his school fees?"

I surrender my list to Tuesday, with the instruction that he is not to pay any more than the amounts Clifford has noted in the margin. Tuesday glances at Clifford's prices, smirks and trots away into the market. The rest of us go back to Celestine's shop to sample the contents of his fridge. In a half hour Tuesday joins us there with my pack full of groceries and most of the money I gave him to pay for my purchases. I bid farewell to Celestine and Atim. Tuesday carries my pack to the market entrance, shakes my hand and disappears into the jostling crowd.

Clifford picks me up shortly afterwards. "So, how did it go?" he asks.

"Well," I say, "it was OK, although I wasn't able to pay exactly what you wrote down."

"Hey," says Clifford. "Do not feel bad. You will get better at it."

Nothing Happens

I hear little Etim and the other boys coming long before they arrive at the house. As they walk along the sandy path they are practicing their drumming on the big plastic water buckets they carry. Their perfect rhythm and complicated syncopation rise to a climax and end with a simultaneous booming thump and a shout at the precise instant they come to my door. I wonder how they can do that. Little Etim pokes his head through the curtain covering the door.

"Sah! *Alagha*? (Sir! Good Morning! Are you up?)" Etim is about eleven. Children here often don't know exactly how old they are. A child's age is reckoned roughly by his or her maturity and not by the calendar. Etim is a skinny, high-energy kid with two new front teeth constantly flashing in a big smile. The top of his head is decorated with a large circle of white soap. Before children go to the stream in the morning, mothers rub a soft bar of soap on their hair, leaving enough behind to accomplish the morning bath.

"We are going to the stream!" he crows, as though it were the most exciting adventure. He says this every morning with the same enthusiasm.

My house is on one side of the school playing field. On the other side of the field are the classroom blocks and the principal's house. Beyond these the village of Akai Isong is nestled in the trees. The path to the stream passes in front of my house then drops down through the school farms before entering the forest.

Outside I greet seven more boys of varying ages. Girls and women also bathe every morning but they have their own stream. The boys are all wearing traditional wrappers, pieces of cloth wrapped around the waist and tucked in, and are barefoot. There are no stones here in Akai Isong—all the village paths are soft reddish sand and are swept and cleaned every week by Etim's age-grade. Etim's senior brother, Effiong, is here today along with his best friend Asuquo. They are about thirteen, both very intelligent and usually full of interesting questions.

We follow the path along the edge of the playing field. Students wielding machetes cut the grass last week and the new growth is a brilliant green that seems to reflect more morning sunlight than it receives. The grass is kept as low as possible to discourage snakes. While it was being cut last week, two cobras were discovered and killed. One was a large Black Cobra and the other was a smaller but equally vicious Spitting Cobra. The people here kill any snake they see since many are poisonous. The venom of some common local snakes causes death within an hour and the nearest medical assistance is several hours distant.

The path winds downhill through small fields of cassava, the staple food here, and enters the forest suddenly so that we are, within a few steps, in another environment. It is cooler and darker and sounds echo as if we were in a cathedral. The favored bathing spot is at the base of a huge mahogany tree. The clear stream emerges from the undergrowth here and forms a shallow pool with a sandy bottom before disappearing again into the dense banks of vegetation.

In an instant the boys have thrown aside their wrappers and are covered with lather. Since it is Saturday, I am in no hurry and move downstream a little away from their boisterous splashing. The Cross River area and this stream are home to many of the tropical fish that are common in the aquariums of Europe and America. I have discovered that if I lie in the water and remain still, these jewel-like fish will come looking for food and pluck what they can find from my skin. There are about fifteen different kinds, none more than a few centimeters in length. I drowse in the dappled shallows with these tiny touches dancing lightly over me, occasionally raising my head to look at the children.

They are now clean and shining and all standing and jumping up and down in the center of the stream in a game they have invented. Their happy laughter rings in the forest gallery above like another kind of bird song. Through the boys' legs I suddenly catch a glimpse of something moving. I lift my head for a better view. Just upstream of the boys I see the triangular head of a large poisonous snake, a hand-span above the water and weaving back and forth as it moves downstream, directly towards that shifting tangle of legs.

I stifle the impulse to scream a warning. It would only cause them to jump about even more and the snake is too close. While I lie there petrified in horror the head moves between the first pair of legs. The boys do not see the snake. It passes between several more legs. In a few seconds that seem to last an eternity the snake weaves its way through all the boys' legs and slides downstream past my feet. Above its eyes are two bright yellow raised projections, like horns. It seems to take a long time passing—its length must be about two meters, mottled brown and green. In another instant, it is gone.

I am totally empty, as if everything that was within

me leapt up to heaven in one wordless prayer and there is nothing left of me here. The laughter of the boys seems to come from a great distance.

"Sah! Oh! You are not well!" says Etim bending over me. I hear him call the other boys over.

"You have lost your color!" says Effiong. He and Asuquo pull me up onto the shore and I sit awaiting the return of life.

"Sah!" commands Etim. I feel the warmth of their arms on my shoulders and look up into the circle of faces. I take a tremendous breath and suddenly, I am back with them beneath the mahogany tree.

"Are you OK now?"

I nod.

"What happened?"

"Nothing happened."

"But you look very happy."

"Sometimes, Etim, it is very beautiful when nothing happens."

Greetings

I have had a quiet Sunday morning doing what I love to do most—puttering around the house and compound. I watered the hot peppers. They are starting to bear a nice crop now, particularly the one at the front corner of the house, whose peppers have an especially rich flavor. I pick two green ones and two red to add to the lunch I have planned—a West African specialty—rice and black-eyed peas with a hot tomato sauce. The pineapples are coming nicely too although they will not be ripe for months yet. They look important in front of the house, six of them in a row, each bearing a small pineapple in the air above the plant like a heraldic standard. I mutter a silent thanks to the previous resident who planted these before he left.

When I have finished in the garden I clean my suitcase. Let this be a warning to anyone who plans a lengthy sojourn in West Africa. Do not bring a leather suitcase. Earlier this morning when I was sweeping under my bed, for the first time since my arrival, I moved the leather suitcase I had stuck under there after unpacking it. During the months since, it has sprouted a vigorous coating of mold, like thick fur in a rich mixture of grays and greens. Anything not well dried and regularly aired will become moldy within a few days in this humidity. After I photograph it I begin what I expect to be an onerous task but the mold wipes off easily. I put a coat of shoe polish on the leather to preserve it from future attacks. By then it is time to begin lunch but I am dismayed to find I do not have any tomato paste. This is sold here in little fifty milliliter tins and I forgot to buy some when I visited the weekly village market yesterday. These small tins are also sold at Junior's store but I stare ruefully out the kitchen window and admit to myself that I don't want to disturb this peaceful Sunday by a trip down into the village.

It is only a walk of some fifteen minutes insofar as distance is concerned, but the incessant and interminable greetings that are necessary here mean it will take at least forty-five minutes or longer each way. There are as many greetings as there are activities and everyone encountered will expect to exchange three or four. If I pass someone working on his roof I must call, "I see you working on your roof." He replies, "I see you walking on the path." I must then inquire after his health and that of his wife and family and crops and I must reply to each of his inquiries as to mine and to where I am going and why I am going there.

When I am in a sociable mood and have plenty of time I enjoy these encounters. But some days I cannot stand the thought of the amount of socializing a visit to the village will entail. I just want some tomato paste. I wish I had the power of invisibility so I could just appear at Junior's store, buy those tins of tomato paste and then disappear until I am back here on my front porch.

As I gaze out the window I see a group of men entering the school compound along the path from the village. Well, at least I can wait until they have passed before I make my foray to the store. But when I check their progress, they have turned onto the path that leads to my house. They must be coming here. I can see that they are the *ekpewos*—the important men of the village. They came to my house to welcome me formally just after I arrived but I have no idea what has prompted this social call. A visit from the *ekpewos* must be accepted graciously. It seems I have no choice but to be sociable this morning.

Anwana sticks his head through the curtain over the door and greets me, "*Alagha!*" The *ekpewos* have arrived, five of them altogether. I shake hands with them all and invite them inside. I know Anwana best since he enjoys my interest in Oron language and often helps me to understand words or sentence constructions. Besides Anwana, the group includes the aged chief's son. The chief himself is so old and infirm that all of his normal duties have been taken over by this young man, the chief's energies being reserved for important ceremonial appearances. Their greetings and expressions are friendly but after they have been seated an uncomfortable silence descends on the party.

Finally Anwana speaks, "Well, Sah, you have been in this our village for several months now. We hear from our students that you are doing a very good job."

"Thank you."

"And we," he gestures to include the other men, "... are very pleased with your behavior...."

I wait for the 'but.'

"But there is a small problem."

"Yes?"

"It is the women. Our village women are not happy since you are here. They have brought a complaint to us about you."

I frantically scramble around in my mind for any memory of transgressions against women in the past few months and find nothing. I've made a point of giving proper respect to the women I've met, since this is not always evident in the way that local men act. I have tried in my actions to show my conviction that women are fully equal to men.

"We think it is because you are from America and you are not understanding," adds the chief's son sympathetically.

"It's nothing bad," says Anwana, "but we are worried that maybe it is something in your religion or something."

All the men nod, again sympathetically, so I venture to ask, "I don't understand. How have I made the women angry?"

"Oh!" laughs Anwana, "They are not angry. They are more...hurt. They want to know why you are so cold to them."

"Yes, exactly," says another of the men and they all nod encouragingly and look at me.

"I still don't understand. I always greet them when I see them. And I don't feel cold towards them. The women in this village are very good, and beautiful too."

"But how do you greet them?" counters Anwana.

"I say the correct greeting, if I know it, and if I am passing close by, I shake hands with them."

"Aha!" says Anwana. "Exactly!"

"Just so," says the Chief's son. "That is the problem. You shake hands with them, as if they were men."

"Yes, of course. What should I do?"

"You should embrace them," says Anwana. I stifle an insane giggle as he continues. "Just a hug to show you care."

"You mean, Anwana, for instance, even if I were to meet one of your wives on the path I should embrace her?"

"Yes, yes, of course. It's not a sexing thing, just a little hug. I will be very angry if you try to sex my wife!" All the men laugh.

"Of course. Is that all? Just stop shaking hands with the women and embrace them?"

"Can you do that?" asks Anwana.

"Oh yes, certainly. I just didn't know."

"We thought it was maybe something you are not doing in America. Do you embrace women in America?" The chief's son is genuinely interested.

"Well yes, we embrace women in America, but not every woman, just the ones in our close family like a mother or wife, or a girlfriend."

"You mean," persists the chief's son, "if you meet a woman on the path and she is not your wife or mother, you don't embrace her?"

"No."

"This America must be a very cold place," he says, then continues, "so you just greet her and go on your way?"

"Unless you know her you don't even greet her. Just walk past."

"Like she is not there?"

"Yes, exactly."

"It must be a very angry place, I think," says the chief's son.

"It's not as friendly as here," is all I can say.

They talk about this in Oron for a few minutes while I dig out a bottle of *kai-kai* I have been saving for an occasion like this. *Kai-kai* is a potent local liquor distilled from palm wine. Drinking etiquette here is that the owner of the bottle takes the first drink in order to demonstrate that it has not been poisoned. A leopard's hair is a favorite poison. I toss off the first glass and hand the *kai-kai* to the chief's son. The bottle and glass move around until the *kai-kai* is finished. The *ekpewos* depart amidst much handshaking and assurances of mutual felicity.

After they leave I again face the problem I have with greetings, only now made more formidable by their visit. At the same time, the *kai-kai* has loosened my inhibitions and increased my appetite. There is no option but to walk down to the village for the tomato paste.

As I move along the edge of the playing field I spy a familiar small figure coming towards me.

"Aha, Etim! How nice to see you!"

Little Etim returns my greeting with his big smile.

"I was just thinking about you."

"And I was thinking about you too, Sah!"

"Look, I need some tinned tomato for my lunch. Will you run down to Junior's for me, please?" Children here accept it as part of their responsibilities to help adults whenever possible. This includes running errands for anyone who asks, but today my request is met only with another big smile.

"Oh no, Sah. Not today!" he laughs. "Today you must come to the village yourself!"

I ask again but he is insistent and joins me as we walk down the path towards the village. When we come opposite the entrance to his compound, I see Effiong's mother near the gate. When she sees me she stands with her hands on her broad hips and watches me. I salute her and she moves towards me, returning my greeting. I make the inquiry about her health and she responds and returns the question. I reply and reach out to embrace her.

She is big. I can hardly get my arms around her but the embrace is achieved. She gives a great shout of laughter and ululates, bringing the other women in the compound out to the gate. These, too, I embrace while Effiong's mother keeps up a shouted commentary. Etim's mother is making *akara*, crispy deep-fried bean cakes, and I am not allowed to pursue my way into the village until I have eaten several. The noise these women have raised has brought others out onto the path and little Etim is running ahead and calling the women in each compound out to their gates. When I reach the next compound I find all the women waiting for me. I deliver greetings and more greetings and embraces. Here *moi-moi* is offered. It is made from black-eyed peas. After they have been soaked, their skins are rubbed off and they are pounded into a fine batter and mixed with palm oil, red pepper and salt. Dollops of this are then steamed in banana leaves. After sampling several of these I move further down the path. Ahead, I can see a half-dozen more compounds and at the entrance to each, several women are waiting.

It takes over an hour to reach Junior's store and by the time I arrive, I have hugged twenty-six women. Weak with laughter, I collapse on the bench in front of the store. Women on the path continue to shout and ululate. I decide to rest at the store for a while before attempting the return journey. Junior appears at the store window and inquires what I want. He is sorry; he has no tomato paste today. He will have some tomorrow. In the meantime, his wife has just prepared some palm oil soup. Why don't I join him for lunch?

I go around to his compound entrance, greet and hug his wife and fill what little stomach room remains with her delicious stew and the balls of cassava flour called *garri*.

I am required to deliver only five embraces on the way back to my house, most of the women being satisfied to call their greetings from where they are working. When I pass the last compound, little Etim runs out and salutes me with his usual grin, "Sah!"

I look at him sternly. "You made me walk all the way to the store for tinned tomato and now I'm coming back empty-handed," I begin in mock anger.

"Oh Sah, my mother told me she doesn't need these today," he says while putting two of the little tins of tomato paste into my hand.

Affiong

Once again this morning I forget to walk carefully around the bedroom door and accidentally stub my toe on it, causing four Agama lizards to tumble down onto my shoulders. The Agamas, both the orange and blue males and the smaller brown females, persist in sharing my bedroom and go to sleep every night on top of the door. The morning shower of lizards is harmless except to my peace of mind. My only consolation is that this event seems to shatter their nerves even more than mine. If I were to react as they do I would run screaming into the kitchen.

When I limp into the kitchen, however, my impulse is to run out of it screaming. It is full of ants. They are coming in under the back door, a river of them a half- meter wide oozing up one wall and along the kitchen counter to where I foolishly left a half-dozen smoked fish. These are completely buried beneath a thick coating of ants. Luckily the small kerosene stove and the coffee supplies are on the table. I advance carefully into the kitchen because army ant columns are always guarded by ferocious warriors that will sink their enormous front pincers into anything that moves. I rescue the stove and coffee and take them out onto the front step. While I sit on the step and drink my first cup I wonder about spraying the lizards with a solution of smoked fish.

Across the playing field, Udong Community School is still quiet as the first rays of the morning sun strike it. I am looking forward to the day. Here in Akai Isong village, a few degrees north of the equator in southeastern Nigeria, there are no telephones or typewriters, but to prepare our students for entry into the outside world our school is offering Office Studies. I have been able to obtain twenty old typewriters from our embassy in Lagos and since I am the only teacher who can type, Office Studies has been given to me and is my first class this Monday morning. Before the arrival of the typewriters two weeks ago we could study only telephone. I trained the carefully selected class of twenty thirteen-year-olds to hold their left hand up with the thumb in the ear and the little finger angled towards the mouth. Then we learned "Hello, may I help you?" and "Just a moment, please," and other such useful phrases. This lesson spread quickly to the whole student body and during breaks, students were often to be seen standing around with their hands in the appropriate position 'talking telephone' to each other.

Nde has a particularly delightful and solemn way of intoning "To whom do you wish to speak?" that causes me and the whole class to laugh. Her best friend, Affiong, does telephone perfectly but has a problem with her little fingers when typing. The rest of her fingers work fine but when it comes to asdf ;lkj asdf ;lkj her little fingers persistently wander off to other parts of the keyboard with a will and life of their own. She talks to them, but to no avail and last week I resorted to holding them down on the correct keys. This worked as long as I maintained pressure on them but as soon as I released them each one lifted delicately up and began wandering around again. Today in telephone we are graduating to, "I'm sorry, this is the Smith Lozenge Company, you must have the wrong number." In typing I am planning to introduce, "The quick brown fox jumps over the lazy dog." It will be interesting to see if the freedom to hit the p and q keys will bring Affiong's little fingers any relief from the tyranny of the a and ; keys.

"What's that?" asks Etim, pointing to the ant-covered lumps on the counter. He's only eleven but is always my first source of information when I need help with local problems. He has stopped by on his way to the stream for his morning bath.

"Smoked fish."

"They will go when they have finished it," he says, authoritatively. And indeed, during our absence at the stream, the number of ants diminishes by half. When I am ready to leave for school, the river of ants is only as wide as my leg and the bones of the fish are visible above the seething mass.

At the school, something is wrong. I hope it is not the principal on one of his rampages to cast out evil. From time to time he becomes convinced that the students are possessed of the devil and that his mission is to beat it out of them. This usually is inspired by his discovery of some new place where the students are hiding out to make love during breaks. But today when I enter the staff room he is there with the other staff and looking very sober.

"There will be no classes today," he tells me. "One of our students has died."

"Who?" I ask, trying to think if any of my students has been absent or sick lately.

"That little Class Two girl—she was in your typing class—Affiong Obong Ntekim."

I am stunned. Affiong with the wandering little fingers, dead.

In response to my protest that she was fine in class on Friday he informs me that she was suddenly taken ill with fever on Saturday and died on Sunday, yesterday. She is to be buried today in her village, Akai Ubon. As soon as the students have assembled we will set off to walk there.

I go home and change into more suitable clothing and by the time I return the students have gathered. Assembled in front of the school, they are subdued, but the only overt signs of grief are tears on the faces of a few of Affiong's classmates. We all file out of the school compound along the path to Akai Ubon. I am surprised at how little organization it takes. Everyone seems to know what to do. The principal explains that they do this a half-dozen times every school year. "Children die very easily here," he remarks.

The giant silk cotton trees tower gracefully over the path and we wind our way past their great gray buttresses deeper into the forest. The students, who usually make a lot of noise when they move in a group, talk quietly today and the birdcalls seem loud and plaintive.

When we arrive at the thatched house of Affiong's family, our greetings are lost in the hammering and sawing of coffin construction and the keening of the mourners. Affiong's mother and father sit surrounded by family members, lost in grief. I am taken inside the house to view the body. She lies on a table in the parlor, looking just as she did on Friday, a composed, good-humored expression on her face. Her hair is still braided in the latest style—many long spikes standing out from her head like a starburst. She has been dressed in her best cloth. Her delicate little hands are crossed on her chest. What suddenly makes her terribly dead to me is the bits of red earth that have been crumbled over her, some on her body and some on her face.

Her body is placed in the rough wooden box and it is nailed shut with heart-wrenching finality. When it is carried out into the compound the students are led in a hymn by the principal.

> *Around the throne of God in Heaven,*
> *Thousands of children stand,*
> *Children whose sins are all forgiven,*
> *A holy, happy band.*

When they begin the glorious chorus to this hymn their voices swell and separate into parts with girls and small boys singing high and big boys singing low. But the open weeping is too much for more than one chorus. Everyone is crying and wailing now and after a few words from the pastor the coffin is lowered into the grave near the house. Some students throw themselves on the ground and others rush towards the grave screaming and crying. Everyone is shouting and weeping and struggling as the earth is shoveled into the grave.

The evening passes slowly. I am too morose to seek company and so I sit and try to read. But Affiong's sweet child's face continually rises up in my mind and her silvery laughter rings in my memory. Eventually I put the book aside. There is nothing to do with such feelings of sorrow and loss but to continue to breathe, and have faith that they will pass. I wander restlessly around in the house. In the kitchen, the ants have gone and nothing remains of the fish but bones on the counter. I sweep these into the garbage and check to make sure I have left nothing out that will attract another visit.

As I prepare for bed I hear a light knock on the door. It is thirteen-year-old Effiong and his brother, little Etim, bearing a sleeping mat. "Our mother sent us to stay with you," says Effiong. "She says it is not good to be alone at night when you are sad. Bad *juju* can come and attack you."

They spread their mat on the bedroom floor and within ten minutes of their arrival they are both asleep. I watch the slow rise and fall of their chests, listen to the soft sigh of their breathing and feel peace returning. I am suddenly sleepy. Their mother is very wise and kind. I turn the lantern low before climbing into bed, and remind myself not to kick the door in the morning.

Night Studies

Deersip devis doesn't mean anything to me. But there it is, in Effiong's science notes under the heading, "Uses of Oxygen." I search my brain without finding a category called "Uses of Oxygen." Effiong and Asuquo have asked me to explain the mystery words. They are seated with three other thirteen-year-old boys around a kerosene lantern in the unfinished classroom block we use for Night Studies here at Udong Community School. About forty similar groups of children are bent over their books around other little islands of light.

Udong Community School floats in a dark sea of

rainforest under the starry African sky. Footpaths are our only connection to neighboring villages and beyond them, to the rest of Nigeria. There is no electricity in these villages although the town of Oron, a half-day's journey distant, has electricity sometimes.

In the mud-walled houses where these children live, one lantern is shared by the entire household and is usually the center of meetings, conversations and evening chores. It is difficult to study under such conditions, so the school has instituted Night Studies and provides lanterns and a quiet place where students can do their homework. The school cannot afford textbooks so the children study from hand-me-down notes, copied and re-copied, from teachers and elder brothers and sisters. This is how we end up with phrases like *deersip devis*. Often I can deduce the original English from the context, but *deersip devis* is an enigma.

Effiong and Asuquo are inseparable friends. They were born within a few days of each other in the compound their families share. Their fathers are brothers. The compound where they live consists of seven small houses and one larger one, all encircled within walls woven of raffia palm. All the houses are built so their entrances open into a large common space for cooking, chores and socializing. Asuquo's family and the grandparents occupy the biggest house. The population is about thirty people, most of them children. Effiong's mother has told me that even when the boys were babies they were happiest when they were together so she and Asuquo's mother used to take turns nursing both of them. The third member of their triumvirate, little Etim, is missing tonight. He is Effiong's eleven-year-old half brother. They have the same father but Etim's mother is their father's second wife, who also lives in this compound. I inquire from the boys about Etim's absence and am told that he has fever. I have learned that the word 'fever' is used here to refer to any illness from a mild cold to a potentially fatal attack of malaria or cholera. I decide to walk down to the village with them when Night Studies are over, to see how he is and take him some medicine.

Unable to solve *deersip devis*, I circulate from group to group, exchanging greetings and answering questions. Every notebook I check has the same cryptic phrase and all the children are dutifully memorizing it. Towards the end of the evening I have a revelation and rush back to Effiong and Asuquo's group.

"Deep sea divers!" I exclaim. "That's what *deersip devis* is supposed to be. Deep sea divers!"

From their expressions, I can tell that 'deep sea divers' means as little to them as *deersip devis*. I describe how a person can walk on the bottom of the ocean when wearing a special suit that is connected by a tube to the surface, where other people pump oxygen down so the diver can breathe. This is a novel idea to them and they are excited by it. It is fully half an hour after the end of Night Studies before I have satisfied their many questions.

"And how much does one cost?" asks Effiong. He is fascinated with the possibility of being under the water with the fish swimming past his face. When I look at him to answer, I see his eyes are glazed—he is walking around underwater already.

Effiong continues to ply me with questions as we walk to their compound. He wants to understand every detail of deep sea diving. But when we are a hundred meters away from the entrance I become aware of a lot of shouting.

"It's my father," says Asuquo in explanation, "and Effiong's mother."

Effiong is still underwater. "If you stand very still the fish will come close and you can just grab them." He catches fish out of the air until we enter the compound.

Effiong's mother, a big, strong, broad-backed woman, is in mid-tirade. She stands over her cooking pots and points at Asuquo's father, words shooting out of her like machine gun bullets. He is sitting in front of his house, looking disdainfully in another direction. I decide to greet them later. The boys take me into the house where Etim lives with his mother.

Etim lies unconscious on his sleeping mat. He looks very ill and when I feel his chest I pull my hand away quickly because he is burning with fever. His face and upper body have been painted with *ndo*, a white, chalklike substance thought to ease fever and chase away bad *juju*. Malaria is the most common cause of fever here. If untreated, an attack usually lasts several weeks and may result in death. Outside, Asuquo's father shouts down Effiong's mother, then continues with a fusillade of his own. I ask Effiong if I can see Etim's mother. She comes in and I give her the medicine I have brought—Fansidar—the best anti-malarial I have. It will usually cure the patient within two or three days. I make sure she understands that as soon as Etim wakes she is to give him the pills with plenty of water and they will make him well. She nods distractedly and tucks the paper packet of tablets into her bosom.

In the compound, more voices are raised now. When I step out of the house I see that although other family members have become involved in this shouting match, Effiong's mother still dominates the group, one big hand on her hip and the other pointing at whomever is receiving her tongue-lashing. Watching her is like standing on the rim of a volcano.

"Let's go," says Effiong. "We will walk with you to your compound."

On the way, Effiong tells me they have been fighting all day. The dispute is about why Etim is sick. Effiong's mother says it is because of the new galvanized iron roof that Asuquo's father is putting on his house. Asuquo's father has lately taken to smuggling in addition to fishing for his livelihood. The extra income from several successful trips across to Cameroon, on the other side of the nearby Cross River, has been invested in a large stack of roofing sheets. His will be the first village house to have its thatch replaced by modern roofing. I've been watching the progress of this roof from my front step, where I can see it gleaming and growing larger every morning when I leave my house.

Asuquo adds, "She says people are jealousing my father's new roof. She says that he is getting too big-head and someone has put *juju* on Etim to kill him and knock our family down."

"And what does your father say?"

"He says that she is a nonsense woman and she should put her head in a cooking pot and make herself deaf with her big stupid monkey noise." Both boys giggle a little at this. I ask them what they think.

"Oh, we don't know anything," says Effiong. "This is for big people."

"They will decide the right thing to do," says Asuquo confidently.

As I drift off to sleep I can still hear the occasional shout from their compound down in the village.

In the morning I get up early and hurry through breakfast because I want to visit little Etim before school, to see if he is better. But when I am about to leave the house, a familiar head pops through the curtain covering the door. It is little Etim calling me to go to the stream for a bath.

I pull him into the room and look at him. He returns my look with his usual merry expression. He's much thinner but he seems just fine and has no fever whatsoever. Fansidar generally acts fast but this is the speediest recovery I've ever seen. I happily agree to join them and greet the other boys outside the house. Effiong is carrying an old bucket with a long bamboo tube attached to it. It is his diving helmet. I notice that Asuquo is absent and ask Effiong where he is.

"He's sleeping," he says and looks towards the distant roofs of their compound. I follow his gaze and see only thatch. The shiny new roof has disappeared. "They had to work all night," he says, grinning. He hands me a small packet. "Here. Etim's mother said to give this to you." It is the Fansidar. "She said to tell you she is sorry that she didn't give it to Etim, but he is OK now."

"You know, Effiong," I finally say, "your mother is an amazing woman."

He looks at me, then looks fondly at Etim and says proudly, "Sometimes, my mother is like a wild elephant."

Mamy Wata

Like a piece of soft black cloth being pulled along an invisible wire, the bat flies silently around the parlor, staying equidistant from walls and furniture as it makes its fluttering circles. It flaps three times around the room and then abruptly exits without making a sound. I am growing quite used to wild animals in the house. The open breezeblocks that form one wall of a hallway allow the entry of both lizards and birds, but this is the first bat I've seen inside.

Groups of students often visit me in the evening and I always make them welcome. With no electricity, there is little to do after dark here except visit or be visited and these African children are very good company. This evening, five boys are enlivening my house with their jokes and stories. The bat causes a sudden stop to their laughter and chatter. When it leaves, they resume conversation, but in muted tones.

"Are people here afraid of bats?" I ask, wondering why they are suddenly so grave. They discuss this in Oron, the local language, before answering.

"Not when they are outside. But we don't like to see them in the house," Effiong finally replies. He visits regularly along with his brother, little Etim, and his best friend and cousin, Asuquo. They all have the inky black skin, slim build and fine features characteristic of their extended family.

"I don't think bats like to be in the house either," I remark.

"We think that when they come into the house they are bad *juju*," says Asuquo. "If one comes in, it is because he is looking for someone."

The boys wait to see what my response will be. They know that I don't believe in *juju*, the local black magic. They are tolerant of my disbelief and attempts to debunk this collection of superstitions, but their convictions remain unshaken. One especially hot night last week, for instance, these boys were at my house in the evening and wishing that there was a moon so they could go to the stream to get cool.

"Let's just go and take a lantern," I said, wanting to bathe but not wanting to step on a cobra on the way.

"Oh no," they explained, "It is not allowed to take a lantern to the stream at night. *Mamy Wata* doesn't like it." *Mamy Wata* is a powerful local spirit believed to live in streams and rivers.

"And what will happen if you take a lantern?"

"She thinks it is an insult and she will make the stream to become dirty and full of mud."

I insisted we go and said that I would carry the lantern so they didn't need to worry about the consequences. We visited the stream and cooled off without incident. The next morning when we went to bathe again, I pointed out to them that the water flowed as clear and clean as before. Later in the day they reported that this had been explained by the fact that I am a foreigner, so *juju* doesn't work the same around me.

I add the bat to the list of animal forms that can be assumed by the *juju* practitioner and curse it inwardly for the ominous atmosphere it has left behind. To combat this, I busy myself making a pot of lipton, the local name for tea, and break out a packet of captain's biscuits. These dry, almost tasteless cookies are thought by children here to be a treat and by the time the last one has been consumed, the conversation is once again lively and carefree.

I have one more visitor before I go to bed, Akpan Udo, the night watch. He often drops in as he makes his rounds with his bell and his lantern. He is infectiously good-natured although he usually has some tale of trouble to unfold. He is father to forty-five children, a very large family even by the standards here, where many men father ten or fifteen children by several wives. Akpan Udo has five wives. He has brought a bottle of *kai-kai*. Tonight he seems happy—his eldest son has returned from a fishing trip with a substantial profit and he is planning how they will spend it to get a wife for one of his younger, unmarried sons.

We share a few shot glasses of his fiery drink and I begin to feel pleasantly sleepy. This is good because I have not been sleeping well, an unusual affliction for me. For the past several nights I have had the same dream. I am lying in my bed sleeping when I suddenly become aware that there is someone else in the room. I wake up and see a shadowy figure approaching the bed. This thing is wrapped in dark cloths with a big hood overhanging an empty blackness where the face should be. I am paralyzed in terror and the creature grabs me by the throat and begins to choke me. My frantic struggles jerk me awake. There is no one in the room but a threatening presence lingers. It is usually an hour or more before my fear dissipates and I calm down enough to go back to sleep, after checking all the doors and other rooms of the house.

I attribute these dreams to a subconscious reaction to culture shock—life here is so different from what

I have been used to in America—and I expect such nightmares will pass as I grow more accustomed to Africa. I assure myself that they are, though frightening, only dreams.

Akpan Udo pours out one more glass and asks me if I will do him a favor.

"Of course. What?"

"Please, I will give you some money and you will send to America and get some of their powerful *juju* for me. I am being troubled here by someone—some bad person has put *juju* on me and I need to get something from outside—something very powerful like they have in America."

"Akpan Udo, there is no *juju* in America. People don't believe in it so it doesn't exist. There is no powerful *juju* there." I can see that he doesn't want to believe me.

"I will pay much money," he says.

I repeat that there is nothing that can be bought in America to prevent *juju*, but assure him that I will make enquiries. Then I ask him, "What is it like? How do you know someone has put *juju* on you?"

"There is no place to hide. You are sleeping, and they will come through the wall into your very room at night."

"And what do they look like?"

"They are just all black. You can't see them, just blackness."

"What do they do?"

"They will put their hands on your throat and kill you dead. Oh! They are very bad."

Each lost in his own thoughts, we sip another glass. Then Akpan Udo departs to continue his rounds.

About three o'clock in the morning my heart races in fear as I struggle awake out of the dream. I am unable to return to sleep.

The following day is one of baking heat and I feel relieved when the sun finally sets. I am sitting out on the front step with Effiong, Asuquo and little Etim. It is too hot to sit inside the house. I am tired but not sleepy. I wait until darkness falls and the black sky is dusted with stars. Then I suggest, "Let's go to the stream." The boys agree.

"I will get your lantern," offers little Etim.

"No thank you, Etim. Tonight we will go without the lantern."

As we set off on the path to the forest, Etim shares his method of walking in the dark. "I can't see the path, so I look up at the stars. My feets know where to go if I don't trouble them."

"Feet!" corrects Effiong.

It seems to work. We wind our way through the fields of cassava, down into the brooding forest, and approach the stream without mishap. There, under the dense canopy of trees, the darkness is complete. Strange bird calls echo with eerie clarity. It is so dark the stream is only a sound. Little Etim takes me by the arm and leads me into the water. For an instant I am possessed by the sharp, biting, snarling dangers that might be lurking beneath the surface and my heart begins to pound. But I lie down and let the coolness roll smoothly over me. The blackness enfolds me and seeps, gently now, into my mind.

As we leave the forest, cooled and refreshed, the newly risen moon lights our path. When we reach my house I bid the boys good night and retire. My sleep is blissfully undisturbed and I awake, for once, a little wiser.

That Cassius

I am quite puffed up with pride. Today I am bringing modern technology and European culture into the heart of Africa—the heart of Africa in this case being our school, here in Akai Isong. The palms, whose sleepy rustling always accompanies my walk along the path to the school, seem to whisper more energetically this morning and my own excitement is echoed by the busy hum coming from the classrooms. We are to see a film today.

For many of the students it will be the first film they have ever seen although they have heard of moving pictures and television. Akai Isong is an isolated village. Visits to the nearest city are not undertaken lightly. Transportation is difficult to obtain and costly. Many adults and most children have not been to Oron, the nearest town, about forty kilometers distant.

I had been wrestling with teaching Shakespeare's *Julius Caesar* to my A-level (senior) students. Then, about a month ago, I heard through the grapevine that there was a sixteen millimeter copy of Joseph Mankiewicz' filmed version of the play gathering dust in our embassy. A week ago I returned from Calabar triumphantly bearing these three reels of film. A man in Oron has agreed to bring his projector and a church in Akai Ukpo has lent us their small generator to provide the necessary electric power.

Originally I had planned the showing simply as a teaching aid for my senior class in English Literature. Jealousy and despair from the other students and teachers, however, inspired the principal to declare the afternoon a general school holiday so that all students and teachers could attend. Shakespeare will debut in Akai Isong at noon.

By half-past nine, the generator has arrived. I worry about the projector until nearly eleven o'clock, when three motorcycle taxis bearing the projectionist and his equipment pull into the school compound. The projectionist explains that the stream was too high for him to drive his pickup across so he had to search for a canoe to carry the projector, speakers and screen. Effiong and Asuquo help him to carry in his equipment. These boys are two of my brightest middle-school students and neither of them has seen a film before. They are wide-eyed with excitement. Each of them stands importantly holding a large loudspeaker, waiting anxiously for instructions as to where they should be placed. Effiong's skinny little brother, eleven-year-old Etim, bears the coil of speaker wire in both hands as if it were a sacred offering.

We shutter all the windows in the largest classroom block. It is actually four classrooms as yet undivided by interior walls. It is the only place large enough for all of our three hundred fifty students and we use it for morning assembly when it rains. With the shutters closed it is quite dark inside. Outside, I can hear the generator cough into life, then gasp into silence again. I set up the screen and position the speakers then go outside to check on the generator, which has continued to wheeze intermittently. The village mechanic is there with his tools—a wrench, a pair of scissors, a screwdriver, a knife, a toothbrush, and what appears to be a crochet hook. He has one finger deep inside the generator. Crowds of students and village children are milling around outside the entrance to what is now being referred to as the 'theater'. I decide to let them enter and find seats. The village mechanic has never been known to fail.

A few minutes before twelve I open a shutter and poke my head outside. The generator has been ornamented with a large tube of bamboo sticking out of it but when the mechanic pulls the cord, the engine starts and runs smoothly and evenly. The mechanic sees me watching and gives me the thumbs up sign. Inside, the projectionist flicks the projector on and a square of brilliant light hits the corner of the screen. The students cheer. I move the screen and he aligns the projector until everything is perfect. Then he turns the lamp off and awaits my signal to begin the film. For the benefit of the junior students, who have no idea what the film is about, I give a brief introduction, trying to explain the story of *Julius Caesar* in local terms. Then I nod to the projectionist and *Julius Caesar* begins.

I have stationed myself beside the screen with a pointer and as characters enter I point out who they are and translate what they are saying from Shakespearean into West African English. The screen is only about three meters by two so this is not too difficult. And it is working. The film is good enough so that with only a little help from me the children understand exactly what is going on. They are riveted to the screen. As an audience they are so emotionally in tune with one another that I am sure they are breathing in unison.

I run from side to side when necessary, behind the screen, to point out certain characters. "This is Cassius—a very bad man. He wants to kill Caesar, this man over here." But when the climax is approaching, I let the film carry the burden of explanation. The audience is in breathless silence as Cassius and the other conspirators close in on Caesar but when they stab him and his blood begins to flow, the kids start to scream. Shutters are flung open and students jump out the windows and stampede through the doors. "*Et tu*, Brute," is lost in chaos and panic.

Within thirty seconds the room is empty aside from other teachers, the projectionist and about a dozen of the senior students. The projectionist tries to console me. "These people are very bush," he says.

In the evening I am sitting gloomily in the parlor of my house, too subdued even to light the lantern. I am alerted by the occasional sharp "pok!" on the corrugated iron roof overhead that the principal wants to talk to me about America. His way of communicating this is to stand in front of his house on the opposite side of the playing field and drive golf balls towards my house. The golf clubs and balls are relics of his golden days as a student at university in Arkansas. I am not in the mood tonight for sentimental reminiscences about fast food. But after I hear that insistent "pok!" several more times, I drag myself out onto the front porch. I am relieved to see that he has shouldered his clubs and is just re-entering his house. I settle down on the step and watch the first stars appear.

I see by a spark of light moving along the side of the

playing field that someone is coming in this direction. It is Asuquo, Effiong and little Etim, with a lantern. Etim sits down right beside me, as if we are short of space. I feel better already. Effiong and Asuquo go into the house, find my lantern and light it and return with my kitchen knife. They have brought a ripe pineapple with them and it is soon peeled and cut into delicious pieces that fill the soft night air with their sweet scent.

"Sah, we want to say that we are sorry," says Effiong. "We are very ashamed because we ran away."

Asuquo adds, "We know it is just play but we don't know how to watch something like that. It makes us want to run away fast."

"Asuquo, that is exactly the right thing to do."

"So you are not angry with us?"

"Not at all."

We sit and finish the pineapple in companionable silence.

"Is he in prison now?" asks little Etim, finally breaking what has been, for him, an unusually long silence.

"Who?"

"That Cassius."

"No, it's only...." I begin to flounder with explanation, then realize what I have to say. "Cassius is dead, Etim. Completely dead."

"Good," he says with satisfaction. "I will tell everyone not to be afraid any more."

Big Snake Coming!

Effiong and little Etim said they would be here at nine this Saturday morning but now it is nearly ten and they have yet to arrive. I wouldn't have waited so long but for Etim's insistence that it was too dangerous for me to go into the bush alone. I need to cut some poles for my yam plants, whose delicate green tendrils are now searching for something to climb. Etim said there were too many snakes in the long grass and I would surely get bitten if I were not accompanied by someone who knew how to see them. I scoffed at this since I know about poisonous snakes, having spent some years in a desert area that abounded in rattlesnakes. I often encountered them in the fields when I was working or when hiking in the mountains. I learned there that they were not dangerous, provided I kept my distance—about three meters. When I met one, I often used to circle around it carefully, observing the way it coiled and prepared to strike should I move too close.

I decide to give the boys five more minutes by honing my machete for the task ahead. When they do not arrive, I set off down the hill into the grassy re-growth that lies between my house and the forest. Etim's caution is well founded in that there is an incredible number and variety of snakes here. I have seen many since I arrived in this area and have never seen the same kind twice, although it has often been difficult to tell from the battered remains what the snake looked like when alive. The villagers assume every snake is poisonous, since many are, and aggressively hunt and kill every one they see.

Finding poles in the bush is not too hard since there are numerous slender saplings mixed with the shoulder-high grass. It is a blazing hot morning and the grass moves with the faint breeze and rustles in counterpoint to the high rhythmic song of the cicadas. It certainly does seem like a place and time that would be favored by snakes but I do not see one until I have cut nearly enough poles for my needs. I encounter the snake when I enter a small clearing. I see its black, glistening coils writhing lazily under a shrub some ten meters distant. I decide to approach a little closer for a better look and move to within about five meters. I still cannot see its head or tail, just a mass of sliding black loops about as thick as my wrist. It must be two or three meters long. I edge a little nearer, remembering not to transgress the safe distance.

Suddenly the head appears, raised above the leaves and grass on the ground. I watch the tongue flick in and out, tasting the air. The head leaves no doubt as to the identification. This is a Black Cobra, a magnificent specimen. I curse myself silently for neglecting to bring my camera. Poised above the glossy loops of its body, the shining ebony head would make a superb photo. The tongue flicks more rapidly, nervously, and the head turns towards where I stand. When it is pointed directly at me, it stops. I see cold recognition in those eyes for the split second before it throws itself with lightning speed towards me. There is no hesitation, no pause for consideration, just an instantaneous decision to kill.

I drop my machete and the poles I have cut, jump out of my loose flip-flops and crash away through the bush at top speed. When I achieve what I consider to be a safe distance, I stop and look back and wonder what I am going to do about my machete and sandals, and my fresh-cut poles. The scene is peaceful, just a buzz of insects and the gentle sighing of the tall grass under the burning sun. But this tranquility is suddenly shattered when a nearby stand of grass erupts with black fury. The thing is chasing me. I forsake the winding path and thrash up the hill through the thickets. Within sight of my house I emerge at top speed from the bush and confront little Etim and Effiong, obviously coming to find me.

"Run!" I shout. "Big snake is coming!"

Etim screams and giggles. He is still at that ridiculous age when he thinks it funny to be frightened. "Snake!" he chortles, "gah! Big snake is coming!"

We do not stop until we reach my house. I sit down to catch my breath, scanning the edge of the playing field where it meets the bush. I wish I had a gun—a howitzer, or some kind of rocket cannon, something really uncompromising and decisive. But when no black head shoots out of the bush within a few minutes, the peacefulness of the morning re-asserts itself and I begin to relax.

"Sah," says little Etim, "you are wearing your bare feet."

"Yes," I say, mustering what dignity I can, "I thought it might be nice for a change."

"I will bring your sandals for you," he says, diving towards the front door.

"No. Actually, I left them down there," I say gesturing towards the gently waving grass.

"Bare feet is best for running fast," he says after a moment.

"Yes."

"Did you cut any poles?" asks Effiong.

"Yes, about twenty."

"You should have waited for us," says little Etim.

"I did," I say, realizing that I sound petulant. "But you didn't come."

"Our mother had some work for us," explains Etim. "Was it a very big snake, Sah?"

"Very, very big. And black. The father of all snakes himself."

While we have been talking, Effiong has armed himself with a stout stick and now he moves towards the forest, beckoning Etim to follow him. "We will collect your poles, Sah," he says.

"Boys," I call, "why don't you leave it until later? Maybe that snake is still there and he is very dangerous."

"No problem," says little Etim, as he enters the tall grass after his big brother. "If we see him we will kill him." Just before he disappears, he gives a little jump and shrieks, "Run! Big snake is coming! Gah!" in perfect imitation of my own warning cry.

I sit and hope they see that snake and that it chases them back with as much vigor as it pursued me. Nursing such vengeful thoughts, I go into the kitchen and make myself a cup of coffee.

In a half hour they are back, Etim in the lead bearing my bundle of poles, neatly tied together, on his head. Effiong follows with my flip-flops in one hand and my machete in the other. "No, Sah," says Etim in answer to my question. "We did not see that snake. But we saw his house and you were very right to run away fast."

"That snake is a very bad one," says Effiong supportively. "If he bites you, you are going to die just now-now. Time only to say bye-bye."

"Thank you boys," I say, for the poles, machete and sandals, and also for their thoughtfulness.

"Sah," says little Etim as they ready to depart, "next time you will please to wait for us, yes?"

"Yes, Etim, next time I will wait for you."

I sit and watch them move along the path to the village, Etim skipping ahead. But just before I lose sight of them, he cannot resist giving one more high-pitched scream, "Run! Big snake coming!" and the last I see of them, they are both running, arms flailing wildly. They disappear into the village and the echoes of their laughter blend with the song of the cicadas until it seems that they are laughing too.

One of the Boys from Home

Christmas morning I awake to the tunk thunka tunk tunk of drums outside my window. These are not the big booming drums usual at festivities here but the rhythms are as sure and complex. Children's voices carry a melody that floats on top of the drumming. I quickly dress and go to the front door. Outside the house is a small band of boys. One of them is masked. The wooden mask is not the horrifying monster mask typical of the adult ekpo masquerades but instead is a serene, beatific face, painted in bright orange and blue. Long swathes of golden raffia, tied all round the mask like hair, hang down to the dancer's waist and swing and sway as he dances. This is the *ekong* masquerade.

The group consists of the masked dancer, three drummers and four more boys, ranging in age from about five to twelve. Clothing in this climate is worn only for social reasons and this group provides a perfect example of the stages of socialization. The smallest boy is unselfconsciously naked. Of three slightly bigger boys, two wear only singlets and the third, a little older, has graduated to underpants. Several nine and ten year olds are dressed in both undershirts and underpants. The pre-teen boys are wearing wrappers and t-shirts. The small drums are made from one liter powdered milk tins with the ends removed. The drum skin is umbrella fabric.

When I sit down on the front step they continue to dance and sing for a minute until they are all facing me. The music ceases and they huddle for a brief consultation. There are none of the usual greetings and I understand that I am about to receive a performance. They come to a decision and launch into another song. The dancer bends and sways in the morning sun and I recognize the dancer's feet. Those toes belong to little Etim, but I know that it would be a *faux pas* to acknowledge that I am aware of the person under the mask.

Ekong is the most important boys' masquerade. These groups exist all year long and are infamous for their mischief. They are supposed to play pranks and steal food to eat while they hide in the forest. They are also called to dance for a woman who wishes to become pregnant or to bring good fortune to a house. Boys stay in this company until they reach puberty. Then they are inducted into other societies that have more social responsibility.

The energy and joy of the presentation make it seem that good luck has already arrived. I have been told that to show my appreciation for such a visit, I should make a small donation for the dancer's refreshment. I pull out my wallet when the performance is over and one boy steps forward to accept the money on behalf of the group. That they are pleased with the amount of the gift is expressed by the increased volume and tempo of their song of thanks and praise, and the dancer cavorts with even more evident glee. I watch them as they dance down the path until they turn into the forest, then I go inside to make my morning coffee.

My Christmas morning breakfast is truly festive. Effiong's mother gave me two eggs last night and I fry these with some potatoes, the first potatoes I have had in almost four months. These were brought to me by a fellow volunteer, who bought them in Calabar, the nearest place where such delicacies can be found. For the final gourmet touch to this feast I open a small can of Heinz baked beans, to wallow in sentimental flavors. As I open the beans I giggle to find myself singing, "It's Christmas in Killarney, with all of the folks at home!"

When I again hear drumming nearing the house, I

rise from the empty breakfast plate and, full of potato inspiration, I bellow in my finest Irish brogue, "The door is always open, the neighbors pay a call!" Outside is another party of small boys with a dancer wearing a pink mask dotted with blue spots. I do not recognize the dancer but gift them just as generously for their music and their blessing. On their departure, they too turn into the forest on the way leading to Akai Udong.

My house must be a designated stop on a route these groups are following between villages.

The third party of boys arrives shortly after I finish washing the breakfast dishes. Some of the boys in this group look vaguely familiar.

So it goes throughout the morning, as I clean up the house and prepare myself to go visiting, every twenty minutes or half hour another group arrives at the door. All the small boys in this village must belong to *ekong* societies. As the fourth bunch leaves, I reflect that the orange and blue mask on this last dancer appeared to be the same mask as on the first dancer. I sit down on the front step and watch as they disappear into the forest on the way to Akai Udong. I will wait until the next group appears.

The drums alert me and I see the next ensemble emerging from the forest, and not coming along the trail from the village as I had earlier assumed. When they arrive I scrutinize them carefully. Six at least of the nine members of this group have been here before and the mask on this fifth dancer is the same distinctive pink with blue spots as that worn during the second performance I saw this morning. They receive their gift and sing my praises with great enthusiasm and good humor and I watch them as they caper down the path and re-enter the forest.

The interval between dance groups has been about twenty minutes, so I give these boys five minutes, then follow them, peering carefully around the corner towards Akai Udong. No sign of them so I move stealthily forward until I hear voices. I sneak into the undergrowth and creep towards the voices. About twenty boys are seated around the base of a large mahogany tree, all talking and laughing in high spirits. Four masks and a half-dozen tin-can drums are piled under the tree. An older boy holds up and waves a handful of money, my donations, and they all crow with hilarity.

While I spy, one of the bigger boys begins to constitute the next group, first selecting the few boys I have not seen yet. Then a dancer and a mask are picked. There seems to be some concern that the remaining boys to form this bunch will be recognized so several of those selected exchange clothing with other boys. When the leader is satisfied that their makeup is unique enough he signals departure and they drum their way back towards my house. I run through the forest and make it inside my back door just as they come out onto the path leading to my house.

By the time they have reached the front door I have recovered my breath and am able to go out and appreciate their display appropriately. While they dance, I plan my revenge for this trickery, and as soon as they have received their donation and gone, I rush back into the house, find what I need and load it into my backpack. With the heavy pack on, it takes me longer than I expected to cross the fields and enter the forest and I am scarcely into the trees before I hear the drumming that signals the imminence of the next *ekong* party. I drop the pack quickly under a bush and run back to the house, once more just in time to regain my breath before calmly opening the front door.

When they have finished their song I thank the boys and ask them to sit down for a minute so I can tell them a story. Little Etim is in this assembly also, as an unmasked drummer. He translates for those boys who do not speak English.

"Today is Christmas."

Everyone nods.

"I want to tell you about a special Christmas *juju* man called Santa Claus...."

They listen with interest as I unfold the myth.

"And he sees everything you do, even secret things?"

"Yes. But he sees all the good things you do, too. And he sees all the goodness in your heart."

When I have finished, little Etim says, "This American *juju* is very nice."

The rest of the boys thank me for the donation and for the story, the drums strike up and they depart once again.

Keeping low, I race through the fields into the trees, grab the pack and crash through the bush to the mahogany tree. There I quickly unload the large tin of Extra Fine Christmas Special Assorted Biscuits and place around it the four liter bottles of soft drink that I have been saving for a special occasion. I suddenly realize that the boys may be frightened by the mysterious appearance of these treats. I quickly print in big block letters across the wrapping on the biscuit tin, "To *Ekong*, from Santa Claus. Merry Christmas!" The drums are approaching and I make my escape without a moment to spare. As soon as I reach the house, I quickly change my sweat-drenched clothes and set off down the path to Akai Isong. I have promised many people that I will visit them this Christmas day.

My last stop, in the evening of what has been a busy and delightful day, is at the compound where Etim and Effiong's family lives. This compound is almost a second home for me and I have saved it for my final visit today because I know that here, more than anywhere else, I will feel surrounded by family and friends. Effiong rushes up to me as I enter and while leading me to a seat, tells me of a wonderful experience that little Etim and some small boys had today in the forest. It sounds like the cookies and soft drinks were well received. I express amazement and even hint at a little disbelief. While Effiong is telling the story, little Etim comes in and, as usual, sits down close beside me. I notice he has an envelope in his hand. Effiong goes out in response to a summons from his mother. She has prepared some food for me. Little Etim hands me the envelope. It is addressed to me, just my first name, and the handwriting is my mother's. Inside is a Christmas card with a message.

"Dear son, I am hiding this under the cookies to give you a special surprise Christmas greeting. I wish on this day that you were not so very, very far away. I send you all my love. Merry Christmas. XXXXOOOO, Mom"

"It was at the bottom of the biscuits," says Etim.
"You read it?"
"I didn't know what it was until I read it."
"Ah. I see."
"Sah?"
"Yes?"
"Next year we will not do that to you."
"But you will come and dance *ekong*?"
"Yes, but we will be just one group."
"Etim?"
"Sah?"
"Merry Christmas!"
"Oh Sah! Merry Christmas to you too!"

Ekpo

I

It is now three days past Christmas but the traditional season in Akai Isong starts several weeks before Christmas and lasts into mid-January. It is the season not only for Christian festivities but also when all the traditional cultural groups display their dances, songs and costumes. Akai Isong is never silent these days. The throb of drums is incessant as dance groups from our village leave and dancers from neighboring villages arrive to display their rhythms.

This evening as I walk down the sandy path that connects the school compound to the village, I can hear young girls' voices singing an *abang* song from the Abakpa compound where little Etim and Effiong live. I greet the men standing outside the compound entrance and am invited inside to see the dancers, about a dozen girls aged eleven or twelve, all wearing brightly colored wrappers around their waists and decorated with beads and flowers. They dance modestly and alluringly, miming hoeing and cooking while they sing. This dance is meant to attract husbands.

When they finish, I make a small gift to the dancers and decline the food and drink offered by Effiong's mother by clutching my stomach and pretending it is upset. It is difficult to avoid eating and drinking too much during this time of year.

As I leave, little Etim attaches himself to me.

"Where are you going, Sah?"

"I'm going to sit at Junior's Store."

"That is good, very good." Etim's face is taut with suppressed excitement. I love to question him when he is in this mood because each question elicits a big grin.

"Why is that good?"

"Because they are planning a nice surprise for you."

"I see. What is the surprise?"

"Well Sah, you know a surprise is when you don't know."

"Yes."

"So if I tell you it won't be a surprise."

"I'll buy you a coke."

"Oh, Sah," he says in great dismay.

"And a packet of biscuits?"

"Oh Sah, that is too unfair!"

"Tell me, then."

"No!" He flashes me his big smile and cartwheels ahead into the night to avoid further temptation.

"I will buy you a Mercedes-Benz," I shout into the darkness.

Etim reappears at my side. "Only one Mercedes-Benz?"

"Isn't one enough?"

"No," he says thoughtfully. "Four. One for my mother, one for my father and one for me."

"And the fourth?"

"For you. You are only a poor teacher and will never have one otherwise."

The two benches at Junior's Store are full but Etim has run ahead and asked Akpan to produce a chair from Junior's house for me. Many relatives are visiting their families in the village these days and Junior introduces me to several men I have not met before, including his uncle. There is a family resemblance but the uncle has the extra flesh that is a sign of prosperity in this area.

Uncle's shining Peugeot 504 is parked in Junior's compound. A car is a rare sight in Akai Isong but during the dry season it is possible to drive into the village.

When introductions are complete and I have a large beer in my hand, Junior says, "We have been talking about you."

"Junior! Now you know I don't want to get married."

"No, no," he laughs. "We will marry you, but not tomorrow. This is the time for *ekpo*. And tomorrow *ekpo* is coming to your house."

"By himself?" I ask.

"No, no. The whole group—tomorrow our big village *ekpo* will blaze like fire across Akai Isong, but first of all he will visit your compound."

This is a frightening honor. *Ekpo* is the most important of all the masquerades, the most sacred and feared. *Ekpo* groups usually number hundreds of singers, drummers and dancers.

From other evenings at Junior's store I have learned a little about the *Ekpo* Society. In these villages there was originally no externally enforced law and order. Persistent wrongdoers were punished by a visit from *ekpo* in the night and, if they escaped with their lives, would find in the morning that their goats and chickens had been slaughtered and their fruit trees cut down. The degree of damage depended on the crime involved.

"I hope this doesn't mean that I have offended someone?" I ask.

"No, no. Not at all. At this time of year *ekpo* dances in the daytime and his visit to your compound is to show our gratitude for all your good work in this our village."

"Hear, hear!" says Junior's uncle and raises his bottle. The other men join the toast.

"This is wonderful. Thank you. Akpan, bring beer please. Some of these men are looking dry."

Junior fills me in on the details. *Ekpo* will come to my house early in the morning, about seven o'clock. I should have a small money offering ready and a bottle of *kai-kai* for the dancers. While we chat Junior dandles his youngest daughter on his knees. This little Akpa is a delight, about three years old, with a perfectly round face and a perpetual smile. Junior loves both his daughters and his baby son but there is a special bond between him and this daughter that is charming to behold.

"My wife wishes you to photograph her and the children tomorrow afternoon," says Junior. "Can you do that? They will be wearing their new Christmas dresses."

I agree and we set a time.

The conversation, largely in English for my benefit, becomes more general but soon turns to government corruption, a favorite topic amongst Nigerians. Junior's uncle works in the state capitol, Calabar, and has a wealth of stories about the scams practiced there with the public money and the bribes the big men pay to escape punishment for their graft.

"It sounds like business," I say, "but a different kind of business."

"Fine, fine," says Junior's uncle. "If only business, then OK, but these big men can do anything they want, even murder."

"Yes, yes," says Junior, "like that Okoroki."

The other men nod their agreement.

"This Okoroki," explains Junior's uncle, "he had so many big contracts from the government since his brother was a minister, and he sold them all off to subcontractors for big money. They say he has a container—you know, one of those big steel boxes like a house—this container is full of money, buried in his compound."

"But about his wife," urges Junior.

"It was in Umuahia, in a big hotel there. Okoroki was heard shouting at his wife and beating her. They were on the fifth floor of the hotel. She runs out onto the balcony and he chases her and continues shouting and beating on her in full view of all the hawkers and people on the street below in front of the hotel. Everyone is watching. In his rage he grabs her and throws her off the balcony. She is smashed dead. Hundreds of people saw him lift her up and throw her over and the next day, the newspapers reported it as a tragic accident, saying she tripped and fell over the railing. Okoroki went completely free and everyone was even afraid to say anything."

"But her family were not small people either," says one of the other men.

"No, it cost him a lot of money, some say a million naira, to make them forget her. And nearly that much to the police too. But for Okoroki, it's just pocket money.

He doesn't even have to open his container for those little millions."

The talk moves on to local politics and I ponder how quickly I have grown used to always being included in any discussion that takes place when I am near, not just here at Junior's store but anywhere in this village. If the discussion is in Oron language people will either switch to English for my benefit or someone will take it upon himself to translate for me so that I never feel left out. As I finish my second beer I recollect that I must be up early the next day for *Ekpo* and I bid the men goodnight.

"So," I say to Etim when we are walking homeward along the sandy, moonlit path, "you got to keep your secret and I bought you a coke anyway. Was that a surprise?"

"Oh, no, Sah. That was not a surprise. I knew you would give me a coke."

"But maybe I was angry."

"Sah, you are never angry. In fact, you are too good. We want to keep you here always." He runs off into his compound leaving me to blush my way home.

II

"Sah! They are coming!" Etim pokes his head through the bedroom window. I have overslept but dress quickly and join Etim and Effiong on the front step just as a milling, thumping crowd becomes visible spilling out onto the path from the village. There must be at least ten drummers and the beat is fast and ominous. There is power here and the warm morning air seems to swell and contract with the drumbeats like a giant beast breathing. Leading the way, about twenty men dance while throwing cutlasses high into the air and catching them. The spinning blades gleam and sparkle in the morning sunlight. A dense mass of people dance and sing behind these men and surround a pitch black figure wearing a huge devilish mask. This is *ekpo*. The singing and writhing of this crowd is hypnotic. Little Etim is jumping up and down.

"Oh, Sah, this our *ekpo* is too sweet!" He cuts across the playing field at a run and disappears into the vibrating throng. I am glad that Effiong remains with me.

When they reach my house, those in front of *ekpo* part and I can see that he dances alone in the center of a circle. There is thick rope around his waist. Tied to it are four long tethers with men at the end of each one. *Ekpo* is dangerous; he is madness incarnate and slashes his cutlass this way and that, only restrained from slaughtering nearby dancers by the four men with the ropes. The crowd surges and screams when he gets too close but the singing never ceases and the drums pound without missing a beat.

The *ekpo* mask is truly frightening. Its large, hollow eyes and bared teeth signal insane rage. The mouth is articulated but the voice that issues is a subhuman growl or a high mad wailing song. Below the eyes, two electric yellow lines run down the cheeks. It is said that ekpo weeps when he is unleashed. He cries with the pain and sorrow of inflicting justice, but the tear trails do not soften this implacable mask.

Ekpo dances like one possessed. The drums mount to a climax and then all fall silent at the same instant and the throng gives a joyous shout. One of the dancers accompanying *ekpo* comes towards me waving a freshly honed matchete. Effiong nudges me.

I step forward a little fearfully, holding out the money and the bottle of *kai-kai*. *Ekpo* makes a lunge towards me but is held back by the ropes. The *kai-kai* and the gift are accepted by the other dancer. All the women ululate high and shrill and the crowd bursts into a new song and begins to dance. *Ekpo* shudders and shakes and cuts the air with his gleaming blade and the swarm, like an enormous sinuous monster, turns back towards the village, with the black, malevolent figure capering and staggering in the heart of it.

I am exhausted, although the entire event has taken less than twenty minutes. As the last stragglers disappear beyond the school, I slump down onto the front step. Effiong appears with a cup of coffee and says, "Sah, I must go. They are dancing our compound now."

I thank him for the coffee and watch while he races across the field. I feel envious that there is nothing in my own culture that has this power and is so attractive, even to children, that they cannot resist taking part. And I feel blessed, as if Africa herself has arisen to give me this gift, this vision of a society at one with its culture.

In the afternoon, after checking that I have film and good batteries in my camera, I set out for Junior's Store and the promised photo session with his family. The school compound is deserted and the only sign of the season is the murmur of drums from the direction of Akai Udong. When I am about one quarter of the way across the playing field I see a figure emerging from the bush and capering along a path that intersects with the one I am on. It is the *ekpo* dancer, alone and unrestrained. His evil mask shakes and quivers as he weaves and cavorts towards me. A high, manic song accompanies his drunken dancing and his cutlass flashes and gleams in slashing arcs. We are definitely going to meet in the center of the playing field. When we are within a few paces of each other I step to the right to go around the dancer. He lunges across my path and drives his cutlass into the turf between my feet. The electric yellow tear furrows seem to vibrate against the ebony mask. I am scared, so I laugh and the insane singing also turns to laughter. The devil mask leans towards me, then one hand lifts it up enough to show me Junior's smiling face.

"Excuse me, Sah," he giggles. "I am just playing my culture."

"You are playing it very well. Here I am, on my way to photograph your family and you almost made me wet myself."

"Oh, very good! Very correct! Thank you, Sah! Our group will be down in the village in about an hour. I will see you later." He drops the mask back over his face, resumes his lunatic song and reels away down the path that leads to Akai Udong.

A few minutes later I am in Junior's compound. This downtown part of Akai Isong is crowded and busy this afternoon. A large women's *abang* group is dancing and singing in the compound next to Junior's while across the path, the packed village church pulses with the drums that accompany its services. Villagers and visitors wander to and fro in groups, everyone dressed in the bright new clothes that mark the season.

After finding me a seat and instructing Akpan to provide me with a beer, Junior's wife hustles the children into the house to dress them for the photographs. Generally I am not too fond of taking formal photos of these villagers because everyone stands stiffly and wears an expression of deep gravity and gloom. With Junior's family, however, I know that little Akpa's irrepressible smile will make the photos worthwhile.

The children are gorgeous. Akpa wears a pink and white dress decorated with white lace and red cloth roses. Her small feet bear matching white socks trimmed with little roses and shining black patent leather shoes. Her older sister, mother and baby brother are all dressed in matching cloth, a bold design of cowrie shells in red and black against a dark green background. I shoot them as a group in several different arrangements and then take portrait shots of each of them. A request comes from the women's group that I photograph them while they perform so, when I have finished with Junior's family, we all walk out into the road where the *abang* dancers are performing before a large crowd.

I move around to get the sun behind me and see that Junior's family has joined the dance group, even Akpa turning and twisting joyfully to the rhythm. I slip on the telephoto lens and focus in on her. Suddenly there is the sound of a car engine very loud. Someone shrieks above the drumming and a big, black Mercedes-Benz hurtles into the crowd. People scatter in all directions, but above them, like a rag doll thrown into the air, spins little Akpa. She lands with a thump just in front of me. I lean over to help her up but one glance tells me she is dead, all the joyous, bouncing life in her punched out in an instant.

Junior's wife gathers little Akpa in her arms, throws her head back and wails. Her keening cuts through the yelling chaos like a razor. Other women begin to scream. I see the driver's car door open and a large, fat man lurches out, a bottle of gin in one hand. He leans drunkenly against the fender. Several men are shouting and pushing against him. The confusion of people raging and screaming is suddenly shattered again by the clang of metal against metal as a machete slashes the hood of the car. *Ekpo* is here.

The cutlass rises again and arcs down across the driver's neck, his stupid, drunken face only beginning to register concern as his head topples off his shoulders onto the ground like a cabbage. Blood spouts from his neckless torso as his body sinks beneath the smashing blade. Someone is pulling at my sleeve. It is little Etim.

"Sah, it is not good for you to be here. Come!" He pulls me away into the trees behind the church and along a small path that runs behind the compounds near the school. We make our way quickly and in silence, stopping only once to look back when a dull whump momentarily hushes the screaming and shouting. Above the compound roofs and trees rises a black cloud of smoke.

"They are burning that evil thing," says Etim.

At my house, we collapse on the stairs in silence. For some time we stare at the red earth at our feet.

"Oh, Etim," I finally say. "This is a terrible thing. Little Akpa...." and here we both cry quietly. "And Junior," I continue, "what will they do to Junior now?"

"Sah?"

"What he did to the driver. That *ekpo* was Junior. I recognized the mask. I saw him earlier today in the playing field here and he lifted the mask so we could talk."

"Sah!" Etim's face, wet with tears, is turned to mine. He speaks with an intense certainty. "Sah, it was not Junior. It was *ekpo*." We stare at each other for a few moments, then he rises. "I will make you some coffee."

The coffee is too sweet, of course. Etim is a firm believer in super-saturation. But it tastes good and the extra sweetness seems to help to bring the world back into focus. We drink it silently and when we have finished, Etim takes the cups away and washes them.

"Sah, I must go to our compound now. My mother will be afraid for me."

"Yes, of course. Thank you Etim."

"Sah?"

I look up at him where he has paused by the door and meet a gaze of such intensity that I have to look away. It is the second time today I have seen the naked face of Africa.

"I will come and see you later," he says and I listen to the soft patter of his bare feet trotting away.

I sit on the front step of my house and watch the curl of black smoke rise above the bronze thatches and greenery of the village.

Late in the afternoon, I hear motorcycles outside the house. Four police officers dismount and come inside. One is the Chief Inspector from Oron. I have met him previously and liked him. He is not an Oron native but is from the nearby Ibibio area and speaks and understands the Oron language well. He seems sympathetic to the local people. While he talks to me the other three officers wander around the house, examining my papers and belongings.

"This is a very bad thing," says the Inspector.

I agree.

"This is the kind of thing that spoils this our Nigeria, that makes us look like savages."

I nod, not because I agree but because I want to appear agreeable.

"These people here don't understand we can't have this kind of thing, we can't have this kind of bush thing."

I nod glumly.

"You are teaching English here, isn't it?"

"Yes, and Mathematics."

"But you know, you are from America, where these things don't happen. It is important, more important than English that these people should begin to understand how to live like civilized people. They have to understand about law and order. That is what they need to learn."

I can't think of any appropriate response so I wait for him to continue.

"What happened this afternoon?" he asks.

I describe the photo session and the women's dance group. "Then the car just appeared out of nowhere and crashed into the crowd."

"And then?"

"Then I was trying to see if I could do anything for the child who was killed and everyone was shouting and screaming and running around. It was impossible to see what was happening."

"But what of the driver of the car? You must have seen what happened. The man was an Assistant Permanent Secretary in the Ministry of Industry, an important man, a father himself with four children. Tell us what happened when the *ekpo* dancer came."

"I only saw a crowd around the man."

"And the *ekpo*?"

"Yes, I think I remember seeing an *ekpo*, but there were many people, very angry, of course."

"But the *ekpo*? Who was the *ekpo*? You have been here long enough to know these things. Tell me now."

"I don't know. I'm sorry. These dancers all look the same to me. I have no idea who was involved."

"Think about it. These local people will tell us nothing. This burning car and chopped up man just dropped out of the sky! But you, you know about due process and real justice. You can't see this kind of thing and just say OK. Tell us the truth now."

"Inspector, the only truth I know is that it was *ekpo*. I wish I could help you more. I wish that it had never happened."

The Inspector sits in silence for a few minutes then sighs and rises. They leave the school compound and I stand in front of my house and listen until I hear the thrum of their motorcycles disappear beyond Uduko towards Oron.

Little Etim and Effiong materialize out of the darkness. "Our mother wishes you to come and eat with us," says Effiong.

I beg off, explaining that I'm not hungry.

Etim links his arm through mine. "Sah," he says, "She says you MUST come and eat with us. Let us go now."

We walk in silence through the evening as the stars begin to shine in the purple sky overhead. The air here is so humid that the stars don't twinkle; each one is just a bright warm glow. Etim tells me we will bury little Akpa tomorrow, in the morning.

Expo

I have always loved getting up on Saturday mornings with the whole weekend stretching invitingly before me. Here in the rainforest of southeastern Nigeria, in my house on the Udong Community School compound, I do not consider mowing the lawn. There is no lawn. My compound is landscaped in the scorched earth style preferred here. The flat bare ground is not inviting to snakes and is swept early every weekday morning by students. Akpan keeps it clean on weekends and during school holidays. In the midst of the luxuriant greenery that normally fills every vacant space, this smooth brown area is oddly attractive. Nor do I plan a trip to the mall or supermarket. Neither is to be found within hundreds of kilometers. While I drink my morning coffee and ponder whether to weed the peppers or transplant some banana suckers, there is a knock on the door. A small boy informs me that the principal of our school wishes to speak to me in his office, across the playing field from my house.

When I arrive at the principal's office, he hands me a sheet of paper. It is in my handwriting. "And here's some copies we have recovered," he says, sliding two more sheets over his desk. The original is a draft version of my final examination in English that students are to write next week. "Of course, we don't know how many more copies there are, so...."

"Yes, I understand. I'll have to do a completely new exam. But who...."

"We don't know," says the principal and meditates while tapping a ruler on his desk, "not yet. But we will find out. The boys we discovered with these papers are lying, of course. They say they found them."

"That's impossible. I would never just throw a draft exam away before the exam. It should still be in my desk at home."

"You have no suspicions?"

"No, I can't think of anyone."

"You didn't notice that it was missing?"

"No. After I completed this draft, I made a clean

copy to give to the typist on Monday and put them both in my desk drawer. I haven't looked at them since."

"When was that?"

"Last Wednesday afternoon."

"And who's been in your house since then?"

"Oh, many students. You know I had a small end-of-term party for my class on Friday."

"What about those boys that are always hanging around your compound, Effiong and Asuquo, and that little one?"

"Oh, I'd never suspect them. They're very good boys. This is far more likely to be someone who doesn't know me well. It could just as easily be any of the students in my class. And I often leave the door unlocked when I am out. It could be almost anyone."

With a look of profound contemplation on his face, the principal taps the ruler, then places it on his desk and looks at me over tented fingers. "This kind of expo is very serious," he says. Expo is the term for leaked exam papers. "We must nip it in the butt!"

"Yes, get to the bottom of it," I add in support.

He puts both hands palms down on his desk with careful precision and rises. "I will keep you informed of any new developments."

This is distressing. Never before has anything been taken from my house. I cannot imagine any of my students doing such a thing, yet it is clear that someone has. Theft always leaves such a sense of betrayal. Someone I trusted has taken advantage of me. At home I put these sad thoughts aside and begin to draw up another exam. Three hours later I am summoned once again to the principal's office. He motions me to sit down.

"We have found the culprit," he says gravely. "And I'm sorry. I know it is going to hurt you to find out who it is."

"Who?"

"Effiong Abakpa Antai."

This does hurt. This is Effiong, little Etim's big brother, a boy I would trust with anything. I cannot believe it. "There must be some mistake. Effiong would never do such a thing."

"No, there's no mistake. Those other boys eventually told me they got the paper from Effiong. I went to see him and he confessed to stealing it from your house."

"But he's a top student! He has no need to steal an exam paper before the exam."

"Oh, these boys are too bad. They will steal anything. You must punish him severely or you will never be safe from any of them again."

We sit in silence for a few minutes.

"Or, if you prefer, I can just expel him and we can refer the matter to the police."

"No, no. Just give me a little time to think about it."

"Of course. But don't take too long. We want to resolve this matter as quickly as possible."

I go home to think, but as the day wears on I continue to feel miserable without coming up with any solution. When Effiong arrives in the late afternoon I am relieved to see him, but not happy. He comes into the parlor and kneels on the floor in front of me.

"Sah, I am very sorry for what I have done."

I look at him and suddenly I am so hurt and angry I want to beat him. How could he do this to me? I have got nearly through an entire school year without punishing a single child, without once raising my voice in anger, in an environment where other teachers find it necessary to inflict corporal punishment every day.

I ease the story out of him. He didn't want to steal the paper but many other students pressured him because he was free to come into my house and visited often.

"They said, 'We are your brothers. Who is this *mbatang*? He is here now but in another year he will be gone and you will never see him again. He doesn't need anything from you but we need your help if we are to pass these exams. It's only a piece of paper, not like stealing his camera or money.'"

They are right, of course. I will be gone in a year. Effiong will have to live with his fellow students in these seven villages for the rest of his life. While they may not be his brothers in the English sense of the word, they are in the African sense and many are related to him. In important ways his future happiness will depend on the relationships he builds and strengthens during this time.

"You had to do it."

"Yes."

"But what am I going to do? The principal says he will expel you if I do not punish you severely."

"You must beat me, Sah."

"Effiong, you know I never beat, and I am not about to start now."

"You must, Sah."

"No. Now go away, please."

He leaves and I sit and brood. I feel even worse than before he came.

In the evening, despairing of worrying my way to a solution, I decide to take some air and go down to Junior's store. After we have exchanged greetings and I have had a chance to sip a little of the warm beer that Junior sells, he opens the conversation with the subject that is troubling me.

"So that Abakpa Antai boy stole something from your house."

"Yes."

"At this time of year it is all you hear, 'Expo! Expo! Expo!' These students talk of nothing else. Instead of studying they just want to steal the answers or buy some *juju* charm that will give them top results. There is one man in Uduko who sells a certain kind of leaf. If you put it in your book and then sleep using the book as a pillow all what is in the book will go into your brain during the night." Junior shakes his head.

"I'm trying to think of a suitable punishment. Effiong is not a thief or a cheater."

"Yes, but it's very bad to steal something from your house. It's not just a school discipline problem. This is much worse. You must beat him severely."

"But where I come from, we don't do that. We don't beat children. For us, it's wrong."

"If you don't punish him, everyone else will punish him. People have got to know he has been punished. No-one likes a thief."

On the way back to my house I stop briefly at the night watch's hut to greet Akpan Udo and seek his advice. He agrees with Junior and offers me a stick he says will be good for beating Effiong.

I fall asleep in confusion. I am determined not to beat Effiong, but part of me wants to strangle him for putting me into this situation.

Sunday morning, when little Etim stops by to invite me to go with him to the stream, I ask him what he thinks I should do.

"Oh, you must beat him, Sah. Very seriously! Everyone in our compound is very angry with him. If you do not beat him, they will, and it will be much worse. My father knows how to beat very well."

After returning from the stream, when we part at my doorstep, I have formed my plan.

"When you get back to your compound, tell Effiong to come here. But tell him first to go to the forest and cut some good switches so that I can beat him properly."

"Yes, Sah!" says Etim and he trots happily away.

An hour later, Effiong arrives with three whippy saplings tied together. He is wearing only a wrapper around his waist. I beckon him into the house and close the door.

"We're going to do it like this," I say and thrash the coffee table with a long lathe I have been using for a ruler. This makes a very loud smack, loud enough, I'm sure, to be audible down in the village.

"No, Sah," says Effiong, "you must really beat me," he points to his bare back, "here."

"But if we make enough noise, people will think you've been punished."

"I must have some marks on my back for people to know."

"I can't do this."

"Sah, you must. Otherwise I can never come to visit you again. Those boys will be after me all the time for expo. If you beat me seriously, they can never ask me again."

I heft the switches in my hand. "I don't know how to do this," I say.

"Just hit me on the back very hard, Sah."

Effiong turns around so his back is towards me. I raise the switch and bring it down on his back.

"Harder, Sah."

I lay the switch across his back with enough force to hurt. He shouts loudly enough to be heard in the village and then says calmly, "Again, harder! About ten times, please."

I follow his instruction. He shouts with each blow and starts to cry and scream, but between blows he continues quietly to advise me where to strike next and encouraging me to put more force into it.

"Can you not shout, Sah?"

"You rotten little turkey!" I yell. "Why did you get us into this? You cretin!"

"Two more," he says, "very hard, and louder please." Tears are rolling down his cheeks. Large welts are rising on the skin of his back. I shout and beat him the additional two strokes. He is crying uncontrollably now and I am hoping that we have done enough. But no, he holds up two fingers. I beat him again and he produces a very full-bodied scream with each blow. I yell some more and strike the coffee table. He screams.

"You twisted little runt!" I flail the coffee table. Effiong wails.

I look at him. He is really howling. But when he lifts his eyes to mine he starts to laugh, laughing and crying and sniffling at the same time. I start to laugh too but he raises his finger to his lips, "Sah, shh." Then we are both convulsed with silent suffocating laughter. Every time I nearly recover, Effiong lets out a horrible gurgling scream, which sets us off again. Tears are rolling down my cheeks now too. When we recover, he runs a hand appraisingly over the welts on his back and nods.

"I must go now, while I am still wounded," he says.

I thrash the coffee table with the switches again and shout, "You brainless noodle!" Effiong obligingly screams.

"You twit!"

"Thank you, Sah," he says and exits on a great moan.

"You're welcome!" I shriek, managing finally to achieve a genuinely psychotic tone of rage.

I break the switches in half and follow him out the door. "You troglodyte!" I scream, throwing the busted switches after him. They flop onto his head before falling to the ground. He dramatically winces and stumbles on the path and I can see by the shaking of his shoulders that I have set him off again.

"Waahhh!" he cries, motioning me with one hand held low to have mercy and stop.

I shake my fist at him and storm back into the house, slamming the door loudly. Then I collapse on the couch, once again overcome with tears and laughter that every attempt to stifle makes worse. Oh! Africa!

Season of the *Tsum*

The kitchen is full of the rich, cheesy aroma of cassava *fufu* this morning. The first stage in the production of this delicacy, fermented raw cassava, has been growing steadily more fragrant for several days now in a covered plastic bucket underneath the table. Effiong's big sister, Awa, has promised to make it for me today, and bring some soup to eat with it. Effiong, Asuquo and Etim are also coming this morning to help me harvest some cassava for their mothers and Awa. My farm has produced far in excess of what I need and more than most of the other teachers' farms.

This is a source of some pride for me. When I first arrived at Udong Community School the principal pointed out a plot that he said I could farm if I wished. Teachers are poorly paid here but each teacher is allocated some farmland on the school compound where he can grow food for his family or for sale. In this part of southeastern Nigeria, constant hot weather and heavy rainfall encourage lush growth and the land the principal indicated was thickly covered with a year's re-growth of bushes and small trees. It had been cropped during the first year of the school's existence only two years before my arrival, so it was not expected to produce a very good harvest. Now my cassava farm is the envy of the village, all thanks to a couple of bags of chemical fertilizer, which has not been used before in this area.

In the traditional slash and burn techniques utilized here, land is cleared and planted for one or two years and then left fallow for as long as fifteen years. Unfortunately, increasing population pressure is reducing the length of the fallow period and yields are decreasing as a result. Several villagers have indicated that they plan to use fertilizer on their cassava next year and I am pleased that I have been able to introduce something that will directly improve the lives of the local people. I have another project underway as well, an out of season crop of sweet corn that is ripening below my cassava field.

Farmers here, as anywhere else, are quite conservative

and look on any innovative techniques with suspicion. When I wanted to plant corn out of season, Effiong said, "We don't do that."

"Well, why not? All corn needs is lots of water and hot weather and we have plenty of that all year round here."

"I don't know. But nobody plants corn at this time of year."

This is an attitude I often encounter here. People are so hedged in by tradition, they no longer think. I suspect that corn out of season will cause an even greater stir amongst village farmers than my cassava harvest.

So, this morning while I sit and drink coffee on the front step of my house, I think about my farm and am filled with the satisfaction of making a difference. I am also looking forward to harvesting the first of the sweet corn today and giving the boys a corn on the cob supper for a surprise. While I plan the day's activities, a flock of black and white birds bank with military precision and fold themselves to the ground. They are the same size as starlings and have a distinctive song, a low whistle that swoops up to end in a high clear trill. They seem curious and several now perch just beyond arm's length, cock their heads to one side and observe me. These birds have been around only for the last week or so. Effiong informed me that they always come at this time of the year and that the local name for them, *tsum*, means, "Eats all."

"If you leave any food around in your compound they will come and not go until it is all gone," he said.

"You don't like them?"

"No. They are very greedy, noisy birds!"

"But they have a sweet song and they fly together so beautifully, turning as if they were one giant bird." I said, trying to inspire him with an appreciation of their natural beauty. These African children are very sweet natured but all of their compassion and affection is reserved for human beings. I sometimes try to open their eyes to the feelings and beauty of animals. Effiong, however, was unimpressed by this particular effusion.

Across the playing field, the school roofs reflect the morning sunshine, but beyond the school, great clouds are massing. In front, they are brilliant white against the blue sky, but those behind shade from gray to the deep charcoal that presages rain. Rain here is violent and sudden. A storm will blow up out of a clear sky in a few minutes. The only warning is a burst of wind that bends the palms, shortly before the torrent descends.

After cleaning up the breakfast dishes, when I step outside the kitchen to throw out the dishwater, that sudden burst of wind nearly takes the dishwashing basin from my hands. I scurry back into the house and make sure that all the windows are closed. As I shut the last louvers I hear the first big drops hit the galvanized iron roof of the house. Within a minute the drumming on the roof is deafening and it is so dark that I consider lighting a lantern. Just then I hear voices outside the house. When I open the door I see the boys splashing down the path towards me.

Effiong and Asuquo are sheltering under large basins as they run. Behind them, little Etim is holding a banana leaf over his head, but throws it aside as they rush through the door.

"It's raining!" says Etim with the same breathless excitement that characterizes most of his expressions. The boys are completely drenched and dripping. I get them some towels. When they have dried off and wound the towels around their waists, we have tea. The rain is lessening and by the time we have finished our tea, it has stopped.

Carrying short-handled hoes and the enamel basins, we set off for the farm. The sun is out once again and the sky is almost free of clouds. The air is so clear that it seems to magnify distant objects and sharpen their edges. Every leaf on every tree is clearly visible. When we reach the field, the boys hike up the knee-length wrappers between their legs and tuck them into their waists. Effiong and Asuquo work as a team and little Etim and I work together, feeling around under each cassava plant to locate the biggest swollen roots for harvest. These need to be teased and pulled out of the ground while leaving the plant standing to mature more of its tubers. The songs of the *tsum* provide a pleasant accompaniment to our work.

Thanks to the recent rain the earth is soft. Etim is particularly good at feeling out where the tubers are hiding and I leave him to plunge his hands up to the wrists into the red soil. He does this while staring off into space with a dreamy expression on his face, and lets his hands follow the roots to the concealed tubers.

When I remark on his method he says, "If I am quiet, these foolish cassava roots talk to my fingers and tell them where to find the big ones." I excavate what he finds. By noon both basins are full of cassava. We take a quick detour to the stream to get cooled and cleaned off and are back at the house by one o'clock. Awa is there, pounding the *fufu* in a large wooden mortar, and the smell of fresh fish *egusi* soup fills the air.

Lunch is a feast. The tart cassava *fufu* is smooth and silky and, coated with Awa's savory *egusi* soup, slides down the throat so deliciously that we all overeat. After lunch I sit on the back step and chat with Awa while she washes the dishes in a bucket in the back yard. She is about seventeen and is soon to marry a young fisherman from a nearby village.

"Awa," I say, "If you were not so fat, I would marry you." Awa thinks she is too thin, since the local standards of beauty insist on rolls of fat. Young girls still spend weeks in the "fattening room" before they are considered to be marriageable. She is neither fat nor thin but perfectly proportioned.

"And if you were not so young and foolish," she replies.

"Yes?"

"I would marry you to Auntie Akpa!" She giggles at this. Auntie Akpa is about seventy years old.

"What makes you think Auntie Akpa would want to marry me?"

"She is blind."

When I go into the parlor, I see a grass sleeping mat has been unrolled in the corner and is covered with a tangle of arms and legs. The boys are asleep.

We still have two basins to fill, for Etim's mother and for Awa, so I wake the boys after they have slept for a few hours and we go back to the cassava field to continue the harvest. The *tsum* have moved to another part of the field but their sweet whistles still resound while we work.

"Sleep with your brothers!" says Etim as he lays the last large tuber beside others in the basin. Effiong and Asuquo have already filled their basin and are squatting beside it in the waning light of the afternoon.

"Are you hungry?"

"Yes," they chorus.

"Tonight we will eat something very good. Sweet corn with lots of butter and salt. Wait till you taste real corn! You will cry!"

I lead them down towards the back of the cassava field where my crop of sweet corn has been ripening. I checked it two days ago and it was just about ready. It should be perfect today. The *tsum* symphony rises in a crescendo like a triumphal march as we near the cornfield.

The corn plants are covered with these birds. Every cob has at least three on it, furiously pecking at the few remaining sweet kernels. I run around in the field swearing and throwing clods of earth and the *tsum* rise in fluttering waves, only to settle again just beyond reach. They have lived up to their name. Every cob has been violated and scarcely a kernel of corn is left.

It has been several hours since we returned from the field but I still cannot escape the image of those flying vermin, the *tsum*, crawling all over my corn like black and white maggots. The boys, full of condolences, carried three of the four basins of cassava down to their compound, promising to return soon for the fourth. I wonder what is taking them so long. Then I see a lantern and hear voices moving along the path at the edge of the playing field. When they arrive, Effiong and Etim are bearing on their heads enamel bowls wrapped in cloths.

"Our mother sent some food for you," they explain as they set these down on the table and unwrap them. I look at the covered dishes without much appetite. I wanted to eat corn tonight.

"We are very hungry," says little Etim suggestively.

"Didn't you eat?"

"No. We had some work to do before our mother could cook this, and we wanted to eat with you."

Inside the dishes are rice and a stew with tiny pieces of chicken in it, very delicious. Effiong's mother knows how fond I am of chicken. I am flattered. Chicken is reserved for special occasions. The corn fiasco begins to fade into obscurity and by the time we finish the stew, I am feeling contented.

"Well, it wasn't corn, but it was very good," I say. "I feel much better."

"She said it would make you feel better," says Etim, nodding.

"Please, you will thank your mother for me. Tell her that her chicken stew is even better than my own mother makes."

"Oh, it's not chicken," says Effiong.

"What is it?"

They exchange a glance brimming with amusement, then reply, "*Tsum!*"

The Bridge I

When I think of the bridges of Paris, I always remember the naiads and other water sprites that decorate their joints and arches. The bridge I cross this morning is similarly ornamented but the sprites are real, laughing naked children, a dozen or more of them sparkling in the morning sunshine. The bridge acts as the gateway to Akai Iko, one of the seven villages comprising the Udong community. The cool, clear water that flows beneath it joins the Cross River about a kilometer downstream. A relic of colonial times, the span now provides little more than a foot crossing and a convenient place to hurl oneself into the stream. Most of its road surface has decayed so that what remains is the skeleton of a bridge. As I pick my way across it some of the children see me and raise the cry, "*Mbatang!*" and come skipping lightly to greet me. Others mimic terror and throw themselves off the railing, surfacing moments later, heads glistening, between the girders as I pass. But by the time I have negotiated my way across all are gathered to shake hands and ask questions. I have visited Akai Iko only once before, almost a year ago.

Many of the children join us as we walk up into the village. Effiong and his little brother, Etim, who accompany me, are deluged with questions. One very insistent boy interrogates little Etim while turning his wide eyes on me every few seconds.

"Sah," says Etim, "he wants to know if you are that color all over."

"You know I am."

"Yes, but he doesn't believe me."

"OK," I say and lift my shirt so he can see my stomach. His eyes grow even wider and he comes over to me for a better look, then lays his small hand on my skin. This delights him and he calls several other children over to share his experience that there really is a human being under that color. I drop my shirt. Satisfied, the small boy links his arm through mine and thus we proceed up into Akai Iko.

We are going to visit Akpan Udo's compound. He

is the night watch at the school and has been pressing me to visit his house for many months. Now that examinations are finished and the school is closed for long vacation, I have the time for such excursions. Effiong and Etim have come along to guide me and to carry a message to a cousin of Effiong's mother, their auntie, who is one of Akpan Udo's wives. He has five wives and, in addition to responding to his kind invitation to visit, I have come to consult with him about love and marriage, subjects on which I am certain he must be expert.

A man comes out of the first house we pass. It is Etetim Okon, brother-in-law to Junior, who runs the village store in Akai Isong. I have spent several pleasant evenings chatting with Etetim on a bench in front of the store. He greets me warmly and thanks me for coming to visit him. I explain that I have actually come to see Akpan Udo. He understands but insists that I first come and sit in his parlor. How can I come to his village and not visit his house, he asks.

Etetim is an abbreviation of his first two names, Etim Etim. This culture does not have many names so although everyone has three names, sometimes two or even all three are the same. Etetim serves me a large bottle of the local beer and extracts all the Akai Isong news from the boys.

As we leave Etetim, I ask Effiong how far it is to Akpan Udo's house. He points down the winding path through the village to a cluster of roofs. I am worried that the relentless hospitality of these villagers will exhaust me before we reach our goal. "We'll never make it today. There are at least fifteen houses to pass before we get there."

As if to fulfill my foreboding, Okon Edet Okon comes out of the next compound and grasps my hands. He is parent to two of my best students and I cannot refuse his hospitality. Another bottle of beer is consumed.

When we make our departure I coach Effiong and Etim. "Look, tell them we have urgent business with Akpan Udo," I say. "I would love to stop in everyone's house along the way but this is really important, so we can't sit around. Moving right along, OK?" They nod willingly.

But the next house proves to be the chief's house and Effiong whispers to me that I must stop there if I am asked. Otherwise the chief will be angry with Akpan Udo. As we near the compound one of the chief's sons runs out into the path and invites us to come and rest in his house.

Chief Akpabio's house is big and cool and, feeling the effect of the two large beers, I relinquish haste and sink resignedly into a soft armchair. I have met the chief before, at school trustee meetings. He is perfectly round with a firm fatness and is fully as jovial as such people are reputed to be. He wishes me to stay for lunch.

I explain that I have come to visit Akpan Udo on a matter of some urgency and I must see him today.

"Of course," says Chief Akpabio, "Of course, of course. That is no problem, no problem, no problem at all. I will send someone to fetch him and he can carry you to his house when we have finished lunch. And, lunch, ah, lunch—I am so happy. You have arrived at just the right time. Exactly! Do you like *mumy abak*?"

I love *mumy abak* so the matter is settled. *Mumy abak* is a soup made from fresh palm oil, red peppers and pounded green leaf. It is unique and delicious. When it is brought in I am happy to see it is being served with *ekpang,* another treat. *Ekpang* are made from cassava and are steamed in banana leaves. They are very smooth and white and have a consistency like stiff jelly. We unwrap the *ekpang* and dip them into the *mumy abak,* then swallow. The rich red *mumy abak* marries the beer and generates warm sentiment. I love the chief. I love this village. But eventually we finish the soup and I realize that, although I don't want to move, I must continue on my mission to see Akpan Udo. In reply to the chief's entreaties that I take a little more refreshment, I ask him if I could possibly have a cup of Nescafé , the generic name for coffee here.

While I am drinking the coffee and trying to wake up, Akpan Udo appears and magically, after sitting and chatting for only a few minutes with the chief, he indicates that we should go to his house. Of course, we still have to stop at each house along the way and greet the inhabitants, but our progress through the village is relatively unimpeded by further hospitality. By the time we get to Akpan Udo's compound, I am feeling alert and energetic.

After we are settled in his parlor and have once again formally exchanged greetings I give him some kola nuts. These ivory-colored nuts contain a high level of caffeine and other mild stimulants and are a traditional gift to a host, much as flowers are often brought by guests in other parts of the world. He thanks me and brings out a knife and a board to cut the kola. While we chew the bitter nuts he questions me for the news of Akai Isong. We chat for a while about the school and mutual friends and then I recall a package I have brought for him.

"Akpan Udo, you remember asking me some time ago for some *juju* from America?"

He nods and passes me another piece of kola.

"Well, this is the best I can do." I hand him the small package. "Go ahead, open it." It is an amulet I have asked a Catholic friend to send me, filled with a few drops of holy water from Lourdes. "Perhaps it will help you." Akpan Udo is bedeviled by *juju* and has asked me several times to obtain a powerful American *juju* charm to protect him. "Put it over the doorway, exactly in the center."

With the aid of a chair, the amulet is installed over

the front door amongst bundles of bones, lizard tails and dried monkey parts also supposed to be useful in driving away bad *juju*. When he returns to his seat, I swear him to secrecy because I do not want to be bothered by a stream of other supplicants for such charms.

"We must drink to this," he says, taking a bottle of the locally distilled liquor out of a cabinet. He mutters a brief incantation and pours a few drops onto the earthen floor for the ancestors. Then he fills and drains a shot glass before handing it to me.

This local liquor is almost tasteless and about the same strength as gin. The kola makes it taste sweet. I realize that before we go much further I should introduce the topic I have come to discuss. A fellow volunteer named Clifford has become infatuated with a girl in his village. He has had no success in approaching the girl and thinks that he may do better if he employs traditional ways of courtship. Clifford has asked me if I can find out about this so I have come to seek information from Akpan Udo.

"Akpan Udo, I have a friend who has a problem and I said that I would get some advice from you."

Akpan Udo nods. "Your friend has a problem, yes."

"He has fallen in love with a village girl and because he is a stranger, he doesn't know what to do."

"And this girl is very beautiful?"

"According to my friend, yes, she is very beautiful."

"Your friend is a teacher, yes?"

"Yes, but this girl has finished her schooling so

there is no problem. He wants to get closer to this girl, to get to know her and spend some time with her. But whenever he talks to her she just laughs and says he must speak to her father."

"Does she live in the same village?"

"No, but her village is close to his."

Akpan Udo ponders this information for a few minutes.

"He is also worried that he is too old for the girl, that there will be some objection because of the age difference."

"No, that is not important unless he is very old."

"Good."

"Usually, we have a woman who does this, someone who knows both families. Then the boy's family will call her and she will go and discuss with the girl's family. This way everyone can say what they wish and no-one's feelings are hurt."

"Yes, but this is a rather different situation."

"And your friend wants to marry this girl?"

"Well, I don't know. But he wants to get to know her better to see if he can marry her."

"And he has no woman friend, an older woman, who can go and speak for him?"

"I don't think so."

"Yes, this is a difficult problem. Let me think." He gets up and leaves the room. When he returns he says, "I have asked them to prepare us a little food." He pours us each another shot glass of liquor and we sit and think. A woman comes into the room. Akpan Udo introduces her as his wife. I know she must be his first wife because succeeding wives would be introduced as 'second wife' or 'third wife.'

"This one is very wise," he says, "So I have asked her to help us. She does not speak English so I will explain what the problem is."

While they talk in the local language, I observe the woman. I have often been curious to meet her. Akpan Udo was a rarity as a child because he was an only child. As he tells it, "My parents were so worried that they might have no grandchildren that they married me my first wife when I was fourteen. They built us a little house on their compound and my father said I was not to worry about anything but just to make babies. That was my work. Just make babies. And my wife was very beautiful so we were very happy." When his first wife began to bear children his parents married him a second and by the time he was twenty he had three wives and many children.

While Akpan Udo and his first wife discuss Clifford's problem, I admire the respect and affection they obviously have for each other.

Akpan breaks his discourse with his wife occasionally to verify information or to ask for details.

"And this friend of yours is staying here?"

"If he is successful with the girl he will extend his contract and stay for an extra year."

"And take the girl with him when he goes to America?"

"Yes, I expect so. I don't think he is planning so far ahead yet. Right now he is just in love."

"And does he understand about bride price and other obligations?"

"Yes, I think so. There should be no problem with that."

"You know that the family of a girl who has finished high school will expect to be paid very well for the money they have put into her education?"

"Yes."

While this information is relayed to his wife, the curtain over the door is pulled aside and Mbye enters bearing a platter of *moi-moi*. I am proud of this daughter of Akpan Udo. Very few girls manage to finish high school here and of those that graduated this year, Mbye is one of the best and is a delightful girl as well as a good student. She greets me modestly in her role as a daughter of the house. As a student she was much more assertive.

Moi-moi! I am still full of Chief Akpabio's soup but *moi-moi* is another favorite. After greeting me Mbye stands to one side until her father gestures to the floor. She kneels comfortably in the space between her parents' chairs and demurely keeps her eyes cast down. I remark on how delicious the *moi-moi* is.

"Yes, Mbye's mother taught her how to make it. Mbye is a very good cook."

Akpan Udo and his wife converse a little more, then he says, "My wife has an idea of how you, your friend that is, can approach the family."

"Yes?"

"He cannot talk directly about the matter with the father. That is too rude. What he can do though is to visit the family and say that he is coming to speak for someone else who is interested in the daughter. He should bring some small gift and some kola."

"Aha, I understand."

"But he must not ever forget that he is speaking for someone else, not at least until the business is completely settled."

"But how are the family to know who the person, the 'someone else,' is?"

"Oh, they will know. But if you were to be obvious about it, it shows no respect for the proper way of doing things, so you, your friend, must always say that he is asking for someone else."

"OK, that's fine. But what of the rest, all the bride price and that?"

Akpan Udo makes a small gesture and Mbye rises gracefully and leaves the room. Then he translates my question to his wife. They exchange significant looks and I am glad I have come to them for advice. They are giving me real insight into the courtship process that will be valuable to Clifford.

Akpan Udo turns to me and replies, "Bride price

and other things are for later, after the first visit. When you come, when he goes back again, they will tell him what he must do."

"And in the meantime he can see the girl?"

Again a brief discussion precedes his answer, "Oh yes, the family will arrange for them to meet from time to time and get to know each other a little."

I unwrap another *moi-moi*. "These are really delicious."

Akpan Udo's wife makes some remarks to him. He nods in agreement, then turns to me and says, "My wife says she is very pleased that you like Mbye's *moi-moi*. Next time she makes them we will send her to bring some to you in Akai Isong."

"Oh, that's very kind, but really, it's much too far just for *moi-moi*. There are some women in my village...."

Akpan Udo interrupts, "No, no. It's no trouble at all. We are very happy. We want her to visit you. She will come to your house..." he consults with his wife, "...next Wednesday morning. Now let us drink." Once again the shot glasses are filled and emptied. I am very satisfied with the information I have received. I begin to plan tomorrow's visit to Clifford. Outside, the afternoon sun has sunk to the level of the treetops. If we are to get back to Akai Isong before dark we must leave soon.

In the compound we find Effiong's auntie and I collect the boys to make our departure. Akpan Udo escorts us to the rise above the bridge and then bids us goodbye. We walk down the path and onto the bridge.

I hear a shout and look back to see Akpan Udo waving before disappearing back into the village.

"Did you hear what he said?" I ask the boys.

Etim snickers. "He says you will please to name your first boy-child after him!"

I am busy greeting children on the bridge for their evening bath and do not consider the meaning of Akpan Udo's words until we regain the path on the other side of the stream. Then I begin to wonder. As we stroll down the path towards Akai Isong I go back over my discussion with Akpan Udo and his wife and plan my presentation to Clifford. But the more I review the afternoon's conversation, the more Akpan Udo's parting words return to haunt me. Effiong confirms the growing certainty of their meaning. He has been silent as we walk and now speaks soberly and sadly.

"Our mother will be very angry with you," he says.

"Why?"

"You should have told her that you want to marry Mbye. She is very good at these things. She would have been happy to make all the arrangements for you."

"What makes you think I want to marry Mbye?"

"Everyone knows, except us. We were very embarrassed today. It is like we are not even your friends. While you were in the house, Akpan Udo came out into the compound very excited. He said you have come to marry Mbye and she should put on a good cloth and bring some food. Then he had a talk with his wife and told her to come."

I explain about Clifford and report in detail on my talk with Akpan Udo. They find it hilarious. When we arrive back in Akai Isong, they rush through the gate of their compound to share the story with Effiong's mother. I follow because I know I am going to need help with this.

As usual, Effiong's mother is surrounded by cooking pots and children. She looks shocked at first as Effiong begins his recitation. But her surprise soon turns to boisterous laughter. The placid baby on her back wakes and looks around in wide-eyed but good-humored amazement as he is rocked and jiggled by her mirth.

When her amusement has subsided and she understands the whole story, she tells me not to worry. She knows what to do and say so everyone will understand the truth and no-one's feelings will be hurt. She says she wanted to visit Akai Iko tomorrow anyway. I am relieved and, as I head for home along the starlit path, I feel even a little complacent. Surely, having got myself into this situation, I can do as much for Clifford tomorrow.

The Bridge II

"I am hearing a bad smell," says Effiong as we approach Clifford's house. He has come along today to guide me to this village and to help me find the house. Like mine, Clifford's residence is on the edge of his school's compound and surrounded by rainforest.

"You don't hear smells. You hear sounds, like music. You smell smells."

"It is a very bad smell."

As we near the door I have to agree. "Yes, something stinks."

A loud buzz alerts me to the source of the odor as

a cloud of flies lifts briefly from a large fish just outside Clifford's door. Effiong holds his nose as I tap on the doorframe.

"Unhhhh," is the response, but I can recognize Clifford's voice. I pull the door-cloth aside and peer into the gloomy parlor. All the curtains are drawn against the morning sunlight but I can make out Clifford's bare feet hanging off the end of his sofa, toes down.

"Clifford?"

"Ohhh," groans the voice, "no. He is out."

Clifford is lying face down on the sofa with his head over the edge. Within a few inches of his face is a half- empty gallon jug of effervescing palm wine. It has a long drinking straw sticking out of the top. Fresh palm wine is a pleasant drink and only mildly alcoholic. Clifford raises his head as I seat myself opposite him. His shoulder-length blonde hair is tangled and his eyes are bloodshot.

"What's with the fish?" I ask.

"Ohhhhh."

"Can we bury it?"

Clifford fumbles for the straw, manages to insert it into his mouth and sucks placidly for a minute. "Yes," he says. "Bury the fish." He nods emphatically. "By all means, bury the fish."

"Find a shovel or a cutlass," I tell Effiong, "and get rid of the fish."

I surmise that Clifford's love affair with the village girl is not going well.

"So, how's it going?" I ask.

"Here, have some of this stuff." He swivels the straw around to point in my direction.

"I'll make some coffee."

When I return from the kitchen with two cups of coffee, Clifford is sitting up and looking a little more alert.

"I really blew it," he says, shaking his head mournfully.

"Tell me."

"I thought I would take the old man a present, you know, sort of soften him up for letting his daughter come over here. So I went and bought the biggest fish I could find. I figured they all like fish so he would be happy and me and Akpamkpa could trundle off and compare notes, maybe get a little …cozy." He reaches for the jug and I point to the coffee. He sips the coffee.

"Yes, right. The fish. So I take the fish to the old man. He does not like the fish. He says the fish is spoiled, that it is no good. Why do I bring him a stinking no-good fish?"

"Good question."

"I did not know there was anything wrong with the fish. The guy at the market said it was fresh. I never eat the stuff myself—it always smells funny to me. So what do I know?"

"Is that all?"

"Well, yes. So much for the culturally sensitive approach." He gazes into the bottom of the coffee cup. "That was my second shot at the gold ring. Total disaster!"

"What was the first shot?"

"I got 'way too drunk night before last and decided that it was all about money. You know, the bride price thing. So I just rolled over to their place and told the old man I would give him a hundred bucks cash for his daughter."

"Just like that."

"Yes, well, you know how I am. Always call a spade a spade. No beating around the bush."

"A hundred bucks?"

"Well, a hundred dollars is a lot of money to these people."

"A hundred bucks, for the woman you love?"

"I was really drunk."

"And then?"

"Oh, he got really nutsy. I thought he was going to go ape on me, jumping up and down and shouting. I was glad to get out of there."

"Bad behavior."

"Yes, he was really out of control, not rational at all. I was scared."

"The fish was more subtle."

"Yes. He did not shout half as much about the fish."

Clifford begins to look more optimistic. He nods, "Yes, much quieter shouting. Not anywhere near so psycho."

"Light shouting, de-caf, fat-free, diet shouting."

"Yeah, much milder. Low-cal for sure."

"And how is Akpamkpa taking this?"

"Oh, she is OK. Nothing bothers her. I was riding my motorcycle through her village yesterday on my way to get the fish. She saw me coming on the path and started to laugh. I thought she would die she was laughing so hard." He shakes his head with a mixture of despair and wonder. "God! What a woman!"

"What did you do?"

"Oh, I had to turn around and come back home. I figured I would go down later when she was not around."

"You must really love her, to turn around like that."

"Yes," a sentimental look crosses his face, "Otherwise I would have just given her the finger and kept on going."

Effiong comes in, having disposed of the fish. I point to a broom lying in a corner and he starts sweeping up all the rubbish.

"Good idea," says Clifford, watching him. "Look, let me get cleaned up a bit and then we can talk." He leaves the parlor and I pull the curtains and open some windows. Between the two of us we straighten up the room and make it look neater by the time Clifford returns. Effiong goes into the kitchen to clean up there while Clifford and I sit down over another two cups of coffee.

"OK, give me the news. What did your friend say?"

"You're sure you want to go through with this? Marriage and everything?"

"Yes. I have to. She is the only woman...." At a loss for words, Clifford just shakes his head.

I give him all the information I got from Akpan Udo.

"Fine, fine. But what I am supposed to do now? The old man will not let me go anywhere near his compound after my last two run-ins with him."

"How about some woman in the village here?"

"No, no, nope. Nobody." He stops to think then fixes his bleary eyes on me. "There is only one person who can do this for me."

I get directions from him for the village where Akpamkpa lives. It is about a half hour's walk from Clifford's house. Her father's name is Edet Bassey Okon. Effiong collects another set of directions in Clifford's village, where we stop on our way in order to buy some kola nuts and a bottle of schnapps.

"Translate everything, OK?" I say to Effiong as we enter Edet Bassey Okon's compound. Clifford said that he speaks some English but I don't want any misunderstandings.

Children in the compound run up to greet us and one goes in search of Akpamkpa's father. He appears a few moments later and immediately ushers us into his parlor. We exchange greetings and some drinking water is brought to us. I offer him the kola and the schnapps and he accepts them with evident surprise and pleasure. He cuts the kola and brings out a shot glass. I remember to pour a few drops on the floor before filling and drinking the first glass. We discuss who I am, what I do, who his relatives and friends are in my village and I give him the latest news of Akai Isong. Effiong is the perfect translator, only translating when one of us looks at him for additional explanation.

"I have a friend who has asked me to come and see you on a matter of importance."

"Please go ahead."

"This friend has fallen in love with a girl. But he is not from this place so he does not know what to do or how to behave properly."

"Aha, he needs someone to help him. His family should get an older woman to do the business. Someone who knows both families. This is how we do it here."

"Yes, but he has no family here and there is no older woman who can speak for him."

Edet Bassey ponders this in silence.

"So, he has asked me to come and speak to you, since I know him well."

"This friend of yours is *mbatang*?"

"Yes."

"I see. This friend of yours is also a teacher?"

"Yes."

"Humph! Sometimes teachers are very foolish."

"Yes, he is very foolish but he has a good heart. And in America, you know, they do things differently."

"In America a boy who wants a girl goes to the father and says, 'Here is money. I want to pregnate your daughter?'"

"Well, no, not generally...."

"In America a boy takes a rotten fish to the girl's father and says, 'Here! Take this fish! Give me your daughter! Go ahead, eat rotten fish, while I spoil your family?'"

"Well, no, not very often, nowadays. It's sort of an old custom, ah, not many people do it any more."

"Kai! America! Big guns! Give me your money! I go kill you now! This Rambo place!"

"Yes, well, he's actually from a completely different part of the country. Not related to the Rambo family at all."

"What of Commando?"

"No relation. The Commando family live near the Rambos and very far from my friend's family."

"And he wants to marry this girl?"

"Yes, yes. I think so. He wants to get to know her a little better, meet with her and talk to her."

"The girl has finished her schooling?"

"Yes. Just now-now."

"I am coming," he says and leaves the room,

returning a few minutes later. "I have asked them to bring us some food."

He asks me some questions about our school until a stunning young woman comes in with a tray of boiled red cassava and palm oil. This must be Akpamkpa. She's like a fruit that has reached the peak of ripeness and is in danger of bursting its skin. She's big, broad across the shoulders and hips, and Clifford is right, she's beautiful, like a blue-black Amazon. The few glances she shoots at me are sharp but full of merriment as well. When she has placed the food in front of us she kneels beside her father's chair.

He and I eat the cassava in thoughtful silence, then he gestures for Akpamkpa to leave with the empty tray.

"She's a very beautiful girl."

"And with an education too. Very cost."

"Yes, a father should be well repaid for giving a man a wife like that."

"Yes. Your understanding is good, but there are many things for ahh, your friend, to learn. And first he must learn patience. You can't just 'ask and get.' Sometimes in life you have to wait."

"Yes."

"And then you have to learn to ask with respect."

"Yes."

"And even when the answer is 'no,' you must learn to say, 'Oh, your "no" is very sweet to me. Thank you.'"

"Thank you. That's very good advice."

We both sit in silence for about five minutes before he speaks again. "What you have said is very good. I will see what I can do."

"Thank you.... My friend wishes to meet with the girl as soon as possible...."

"Yes, yes. Don't worry. Patience. Perhaps tomorrow."

The bottle of schnapps is made to yield two more glasses and then I stand up to leave.

"You will come to visit me again? For your friend."

"Yes, I would like to visit you again."

"Perhaps it will all work out. I will see what I can do."

He walks with us out to the pathway in front of his compound and we part in warmth and friendliness.

As we leave the village I look back. He is still standing on the path and he waves to us. I wave back and he shouts something I cannot hear.

"What did he say?"

Effiong chuckles, then giggles.

"He says, you will please to give his name to your first-born!"

"Effiong! What did he really say?"

Effiong dances away. "Sah! O! You are very wonderful! To marry two women in two days! First Mbye and now this big, big girl. Waw-oo!"

He runs faster than I can and I do not catch him until we are nearly back at Clifford's village.

Anniversary

The first sound I hear this morning is the swish of a broom outside my window. I lie abed with my eyes closed listening to this peaceful regular sound and picturing the flowers that have fallen overnight being swept into neat fragrant piles in the morning sunlight. The sweeper will be Akpan, who comes religiously to do this chore every morning now that school is closed for long vacation.

Today is a special day for me. It is exactly one year since I first stepped out of the plane onto the red earth of Africa. While idly considering this I realize that I have woken up this morning in Africa. For many months after my arrival I slept in America and each morning would re-arrive here, some time between the return of consciousness and first opening my eyes. Today I am here and I wonder how long it has been so. When did the last bit of me finally step off the plane?

"Good morning, Akpan."

"Good morning, Sah!" He picks up a package wrapped in banana leaf and hands it to me. "Junior's wife made some *moi-moi* for you this morning."

"Thank you. And the compound looks very nice, too. Thank you. Are you ready?"

"Yes, Sah."

Akpan has grown and I am looking forward to re-introducing him to his parents today. He has done well in school, placing first in his class. Ekpenyong tells me that he will skip him up to the grade appropriate for his age when the new school year starts. Akpan is excited because we will be visiting his village today and I have given him a little money to buy gifts for his family.

"Did you buy that cloth?"

"Yes Sah, it is very nice. My mother will be very happy."

"When you finish here, stop at Effiong's and make sure they are ready. We will leave in about an hour. OK?"

"Do you have water for your bath, Sah?"

"Yes, I'm fine."

I eat the *moi-moi* and drink some coffee while sitting in the shade on the back step. The sun is shining as brightly as usual in a sky of cloudless blue and, at seven o'clock, it is already hot. Akpan has neatly deposited a small pyramid of the pink blossoms of the Queen of the Night tree in the depression surrounding the base of one of the banana trees, and a light breeze carries their sweet perfume to me. I see Akpan Udo heading home from his night watch's duties along the path to Akai Iko and we wave and shout our greetings.

"I see you going home," I call.

"I see you sitting at your door," he replies.

At Effiong's compound, I sit and take another cup of coffee from little Etim. Coffee is not usually offered to visitors here but since I am known to take coffee in the morning it is always produced for me. Etim is more excited by our journey than Akpan. He told me yesterday that he has never before been, "Anywhere!" Effiong's mother has made some *akara*, deep fried bean cakes, for us to take on our trip, in case we get hungry along the way. While she wraps these up in a square of newspaper, she gives me her baby to hold. Baby and I gaze at each other in mutual wonderment. Effiong appears wearing new blue jeans, his first long pants. A Chicago Bears t-shirt, a baseball cap and plastic sunglasses complete his outfit. It is clear he intends to dazzle the villagers in Akai Ekuyo. He is so cool he is almost incapable of speech, but as I compliment him on his apparel his brilliant smile keeps breaking through the aloof and sinister expression he is attempting.

At Junior's, Akpan is standing beside his bag, and keeps picking it up and putting it down while I drink yet another cup of coffee. Junior's wife adds a packet of *moi-moi* to my pack for our journey. Junior has arranged for two taxis to collect us here and take us to the river's edge. The taxis, two motorcycles from Uduko, arrive as I finish my coffee. Effiong and Akpan mount behind the driver on one of the motorcycles and little Etim and I perch on the back of the other.

Okokon, the *etiubo*, jumps from the canoe as it beaches and shakes my hand. We will ride to Akai Ekuyo with him on his morning voyage and return this evening on his last trip up the river.

"I did not bring my gun today," I say, "but I know you will put us down in the correct place."

Okokon laughs and repeats this for the benefit of the other passengers in the canoe and as we pull away from the shore he goes on to remind them of the story of our first trip down the river together.

I have been seated beside Okokon and while we slide over the brown waters he demonstrates with a pole how shallow they are. The river is very broad here, perhaps one kilometer, but most of it is between one and two meters deep. He invites me to take the tiller and keep the canoe about thirty meters from the mangrove roots that network on the muddy shore.

"Now you are *etiubo*!" he says. I steer for a few minutes then ask Etim if he will take over. I pretend to need to find something in my pack. He steers with such intense concentration I am slightly afraid this experience will damage him. Akpan has unpacked his bag to show the other passengers the gifts he has for his family. Effiong is lounging in concentrated boredom and disdain.

"I really like your hat, Effiong."

An unwilling smile cracks his face, followed by a return to studious gloom.

"And those sunglasses! Good to have some protection for your eyes."

He grins again then conquers it, "Sah, please!"

"Sorry."

The beach at Akai Ekuyo is just as I remember it but this time it is crowded with about twenty children. Now it is Akpan's turn to try to look cool and disinterested as befits a senior brother coming home from school. But he is overwhelmed by brothers and sisters, and happiness and excitement are soon written all over his face. He pulls a little brother towards me. It is the first child I saw here last year. He is much bigger and has now graduated to a pair of underpants. Effiong is looking ferociously bored in the midst of several boys his own age. I resist the temptation to call out a compliment on his Bears t-shirt. Okokon promises to pick us up in the afternoon and we make our way up the path into the forest.

When we stop to climb over the giant log that blocks the path, Effiong is first up to offer me his hand. His baseball cap is being worn by one of the Akai Ekuyo boys and his sunglasses rest on the nose of another.

Released from their oppressive gravity he wears his usual smile.

In Akpan's compound we are greeted by his mother and father. Akpan shakes hands decorously with his father but is unable to resist hugging his mother tightly. Then he retrieves his bag from a small brother and lugs it into the parlor to unpack the gifts he has brought. As well as cloth for his mother and brothers and sisters, he has brought two sets of batteries for his father's portable cassette player. These are installed and reggae music fills the room. Akpan's mother brings us two bottles of beer. I give Akpan's father his school results for the year and, with the boy's help, interpret them. He is pleased when he understands how well his son has done. We exchange news of Akai Isong and Akai Ekuyo.

Akai Ekuyo is known for its canoe manufacture and in the afternoon Akpan takes us on a walk through the forest to see a canoe being made. A large tree has been felled and a canoe length has been sawn from it. This has been raised on log risers and is being carved out with axes and adzes. The humid air is rich with the smell of sawdust and wood chips. Effiong is now wearing only a wrapper and one of the village boys is wearing the blue jeans, t-shirt, baseball cap and sunglasses and is practicing looking bored and vicious.

When we return to the compound there is time only to say goodbye. Okokon's canoe has been sighted and we should go down to the beach. Akpan will stay here until the new school year resumes.

Okokon pulls away from the shore and we all wave and shout. As the canoe noses into the sunset I reflect on what a pleasant day it has been. Little Etim has gone to sleep with his head on my lap. Effiong is determined to sight a crocodile and is busy zeroing in on every passing log and ripple in the water. The sunglasses have disappeared. I recall my first visit to Akai Ekuyo and suddenly something strikes me. I go back over the day carefully until I am certain. Yes, it is true. Today I have not once heard the word, '*mbatang*.' Everywhere I have gone I have been greeted by name. I stare into the ochre twilight in front of the canoe and quietly gloat. A new year is beginning.

II

Cowardly Baboons

"*Malam*! Good Morning!" calls Amina as I leave my house. She lives in the compound next to mine, a beautiful nine-year old girl who greets me every morning from whatever task she is doing. Today she is husking corn beneath the flame tree. '*Malam*' means teacher and that is what I am called in Parewari, a small village nestled at the base of the Jos Plateau in central Nigeria.

I reply as well as I can. I am still learning the complicated Hausa ritual of greetings. First I enquire after her health and then the health of her house, her father and mother, brothers and sisters and, finally, her crops and her livestock. She calls the correct greeting to me when I make a mistake in the ritual and laughs when I say, "Thank you, *Malam* Amina!"

On the road I meet Mamadi with his hump-backed zebu cattle. He tells me he is taking them to a meadow where he has dreamt there is some sweet grass. Mamadi is my best student, tall for a fifteen-year-old and slender like many of the Fula. He seems to be perpetually on the verge of laughter and thinks his life is the best of all possible lives. While we talk he rests one hand lightly on the rump of his favorite cow, just where her tail emerges from her back. She stands peacefully as though that were her only goal in life. When we part he makes one small click with his tongue and the cow immediately walks on.

I leave my motorcycle on the bluff above the river. Today, I am going to follow it to its source on the plateau. Demi and some other children are washing their clothes and bathing. Boi is there with his goats. He asks where I am going. I point upstream towards the plateau.

"You are going alone?" asks Demi, looking regretfully at his large pile of laundry. Demi is also an excellent student, a few years younger than Mamadi. After I have walked away upstream he calls, "*Malam*, wait," and runs up with a big mango to put into my backpack.

Soon the sounds of the children have faded and I am approaching the base of the plateau. The river here is only a stream trickling over well-rounded boulders. While I pick my way along its rocky banks, I scan the grassy slopes ahead because my goal this morning is to photograph some baboons. I know they are here because boys at the river have several times pointed them out to me—small dots in the distance loping along the edge of the plateau.

By mid-morning I am hot and dusty. I stop to enjoy Demi's mango and dig my camera out of the pack. A short barking hoot attracts my attention to an adjacent ridge and there they are, baboons, a troupe of about twenty. They seem to be relaxing. Some of the little ones are playing and adults are perched on rocks, lazily grooming each other, or looking for food in the grass. However, even with the zoom at maximum, they are still too small for good photographs so I decide to move closer. The ridge they occupy connects with the one I am on, about two hundred meters up the side of the plateau. I plan to climb up above them and then down to where they are. I try to stay out of sight while I do this so as not to alarm them

Rounding a large boulder coming down, however, I suddenly encounter a young baboon. He shrieks and scampers out of sight and I hope they do not all take flight. As I come out onto the grass I see they have not fled, but are scattered on nearby rocks, with the large adult males closest to me. I quickly put the camera to my eye and focus on the nearest, but before I can snap the shutter he disappears from the frame. He charges towards me, then halts and bares his large fangs while making a threatening growl. He leaps closer and I notice how huge he is. Several other mature males move in on both sides of me, all barking and snarling and jumping up and down in rage. They do not seem to be afraid of me. Instead they appear to be having great difficulty in restraining themselves from tearing me to pieces. I move discreetly backwards. They advance. I remind myself that this display is just intended to frighten me. But what, I wonder, are those big teeth for? I retreat rapidly and in a disorderly fashion, running and tumbling down the slope whichever way seems fastest, followed by their hoots and barks, which have an undeniably victorious and scornful ring to them.

I rest when I reach the river once again and survey the damage. One sandal and my hat are somewhere above on the hillside and there is a long scratch on my leg from a thorn, but nothing serious. I limp downstream and find Demi lolling on his belly in the shallows. His laundry is draped on bushes to dry. He has scooped a basin in the gravel bottom that is deep enough to lie in. I join him there to let the cool water flow gently over me and wash the dust and sweat away.

"Where is your sandal?" He asks after awhile.

"It fell off."

Demi digests this for a few minutes, then remarks, "Your hat fell off too."

"Yes."

He rises and disappears into the brush, returning a few minutes later with a young palm frond. He strips the leaves and throws the stem away before lowering himself once again into the basin beside me. "I will make you a traditional hat," he says, twisting and weaving the palm leaves under the water.

"Do you ever have any trouble with baboons?" I ask, watching his agile fingers work.

"Mmm. Sometimes they come and steal from the farms. They are very troublesome! Our fathers send us to stay in the fields so we can chase them away. Sometimes we have to stay there for two or three weeks."

"Aren't you afraid? They are quite big, about as big as you are."

"Oh no. We just shout and throw stones at them and chase them and they run away."

"And they never try to bite you or anything?"

"No. Baboons are very cowardly," he says dismissively. "Here's your hat."

The broad, lime-green cone fits me perfectly and is cool from the river. I sink my head until the edges of the hat touch the water and I am immersed in a small grotto rippling with green light.

"And you have scratched your leg. Oh, sorry!"

We drowse for a while in the gentle purling murmur

of the river. I cool my face by sinking it under the water for a minute. The baboons' scornful hoots fade slightly into the recesses of memory.

Demi's finger taps my shoulder and I hear his voice, pitched just above the river's gurgle. "*Malam*," he says thoughtfully, "I think, I have heard that, sometimes, really, baboons can be very dangerous."

Unique Data

I wake this morning to one of nature's sweetest sounds, the lazy early-morning laughter of children. I can tell by the husky tones that one of the children is Yakubu, Amina's little brother. I tiptoe from my bed, peer out the window and I see that the other giggler is Mustapha, from the neighboring compound, both of them about seven years old. They are sitting in the dust under my window and playing a game with sticks and pebbles. West African children do not generally have toys aside from those they make themselves. This game is generating a great deal of delight and they do not notice me. I watch quietly so that I can continue to enjoy this laughter that gurgles up like spring water.

Then, as I do every morning in Parewari, I look from my window across the fields to the rising slopes of the Jos Plateau and feel grateful to be living in such a beautiful place. The fields are a lush dark green dotted with brilliant golden marigolds. The plateau is blue in the distance. A goat bleats, a rooster crows and I hear nine-year-old Amina calling to someone while she washes dishes in the next compound, her high sweet voice as full as usual of good humor.

I am going to spend today with Mamadi and his cows. Mamadi is my best student, tall for his fifteen years and slender like many of the Fulani. He seems to be perpetually on the verge of laughter. In school, I have had him writing a series of essays about being a Fulani. He thinks his life is the best of all possible lives and his essays about his cattle are such lyrical songs of praise and delight that I have asked him if I can visit him today while he tends his cows. His father is the Ardo, the chief of the local Fulani, and has many cattle. Mamadi has been growing his own herd since he was ten years old.

On the way out of the village I see Inge in front of her house loading notebooks and her tape-recorder into her Land Rover. Although she is the only other non-African resident for many miles, we seldom meet. She is much too busy doing fieldwork research for her doctoral thesis in Anthropology at a prestigious European university. Her thesis is about patterns of livestock ownership and environmental management. She interviews so many farmers and herders and counts so many cows during the week that she must flee the village every weekend to visit her boyfriend in Kaduna, there to rest and recuperate until her return on Monday morning. When we occasionally see each other during the week I am mystified by the way her research reveals a Parewari so different from that concocted of my own casual observations and reflections. Since today is Saturday, I am surprised to see her and I stop to greet her.

"Karl is coming down this afternoon to see the site," she explains.

She always refers to Parewari as "the site."

"He is bringing an ice-chest full of Heidelberg and his sound system and generator. You will come over and drink some cold beer with us."

I nod and repress an urge to salute.

"But I must go now," she continues. "I have three more informants to interview this morning and then I will have finished the northern quadrant."

The Land Rover door slams on my congratulations.

I wait until her dust has settled before I kick-start my old Honda. When I arrive at the Ardo's compound and have gone through the lengthy traditional Fulani greetings, I am told that Mamadi went at dawn to the pastures but left Gibril behind to guide me to where he is. Gibril is Mamadi's mentally handicapped little brother. He is a happy child and everyone treats him kindly and patiently. His love and admiration of Mamadi are so evident when they are together that it is almost embarassing. I have no hesitation in setting off across the pathless grassland with him. I suspect his ability to find Mamadi is unerring. He walks in front of me but stops every five minutes or so and looks around to assure himself that he has not lost me. When we sight Mamadi and the cows after a half-hour's trek, Gibril breaks into a run and then stops and looks back at me. I motion him to go ahead and a big smile lights his face before he races through the knee-high grass toward the herd of zebu cattle.

When I come to where they are I see not only Mamadi but his senior brother Basiru as well. I have visited Basiru's compound with pleasure several times. He loves to listen to BBC World Service and is always full of penetrating questions on world affairs. We exchange greetings and they invite me join them for breakfast in the deep shade of a mango tree.

The hump-backed cattle graze peacefully and several young boys perch on rocks overlooking the large herd. Breakfast is one large calabash of fresh milk and another of yogurt mixed with sugar and pounded millet. After we have eaten I remind Mamadi that he was going to introduce me to his cows.

"Let me show you first my mighty bull," he says, leading me through the herd. The black and white bull stands shyly as Mamadi caresses him and points out his especially beautiful characteristics. Then I am introduced to the rest of his animals, one by one, with a careful analysis of the personality of each. We come at last to one rangy looking cow with an evil cast in her eye. "Now this one," he says, "this cow is very difficult. She always wants to have her own way and she is almost never happy." He strokes her ear and she throws her head up irritably. "She is always going off by herself and then we have to search for her. She is a lot of trouble."

"Why don't you just get rid of her?" I ask.

"Oh no!" he says, shocked. "She's not a bad cow, just...different." He tweaks her ear again and we stroll back to where Basiru and Gibril are sitting.

I mention that I had not expected to see so many cattle. I know that Mamadi has only eight and that Basiru's herd totals less than twenty-five. Basiru and Mamadi look at one another and grin. Then Mamadi says, "Today we are taking care of some cows belonging to other people." He and Basiru begin a rapid conversation in Fulfulde that causes a lot of laughter. Gibril laughs so hard he has to lie down on his back.

Barely able to suppress his laughter, Mamadi finally says, "We have decided we can tell you. Some of these extra cows belong to my uncle and the rest belong to my cousins, Ibrahima and Sani. We are taking care of them today because that woman is visiting them." I begin to understand. We are in Inge's "northeast quadrant."

"You mean Inge is going to interview them and count their cattle today."

"Yes," says Basiru. "That spy woman."

"And their cattle are here?" I say.

"Not all of them," laughs Mamadi. "We always leave some for her to count." He dissolves in laughter again and Basiru takes up the story.

"When we saw that she couldn't tell one cow from another we began to move the same cows around from compound to compound. The cows she will count today she has counted many times before."

During sober moments over the course of the day I extract the rest of the story. For months, Inge has been systematically fed misinformation about cattle ownership. Not only that but entire geneologies have been faked so that her construct of family relationships in the village is completely fictitious. Land ownership and grazing rights have similarly been disguised. I am particularly impressed by the inter-ethnic cooperation. Apparently the Ardo and the chief of the Aken people, who also occupy this valley, met and decided that they would cooperate on this fiction. Aken farmers and Fulani herders live here amicably enough but do not generally work together in this way. This complex community joke has generated so much merriment that neighboring communities are jealous. Basiru says the people in nearby Biyor are planning to ask Inge to go there and research them when she is finished here.

"But why?" I eventually ask.

Basiru answers at length. "When you came it was because we had asked for a teacher. We know what you are. But we didn't ask her to come and we don't know what she is. She asks many foolish questions. But she also asks many questions we would not answer except to our friends. She wants to collect much information about us and we think it is safer for us if she doesn't know the truth. If the government knows how many cattle we have, will they not try to take some from us?" He pauses for a moment, then adds, "Besides, she is a very foolish woman and has no heart for us."

We follow the cattle back to the Ardo's compound at sunset. There are no sounds but the clicks and high whistles the herdboys use to guide the cows. I regretfully refuse supper with the Ardo. Fulani rice and beans with butter are delicious but I have been invited to Amina's compound tonight to celebrate the christening of her new baby brother. As my motorcycle thrums through the warm evening I try to think if there is any way I can alert Inge to what is happening without betraying the trust of my Fulani friends.

At home I have scarcely time to throw some water on my face and don a jacket and tie before Amina and Yakubu are at the door. They are a treat. Nine-year-old Amina is always beautiful but in her yellow satin dress and matching hair ribbons she is stunning. The little high-heeled shoes she totters on are also yellow. Yakubu is wearing big shiny shoes and a bright blue suit with a red bow tie. We walk across to their compound together. They each hold one of my hands since neither of them is walking very well.

Within the compound walls I see many guests in the lantern light. The men are wearing the voluminous formal robes called baba riga and the women are wrapped in their finest cloths and crowned with ornate headties. I know many of the people here. Their children are my students and I have visited their compounds. It takes me a half hour to greet everyone properly. Amina's father has rented some plastic chairs and seats me in one of these next to several village men I know. One of my students, an Aken boy called Demi, is sitting here beside his father and uncle.

The men are drinking some of the local alcoholic beverage. It is made from fermented grass seed and is served in a large calabash with a smaller gourd spoon. The spoon is useful because this beer is thick, like gruel, but it tastes good and settles pleasantly in my empty stomach. Demi's uncle is a hunter and he wants me to go hunting with him one day. Demi translates while we chat and spoon the gruel.

The surrounding buzz of conversation dips for a moment and when I look up I see that Inge and a large, bronzed young man have entered the compound. Both are wearing tank-tops, short shorts and robust hiking boots. They greet Amina's father. Then Inge catches sight of me, waves and heads in my direction, pulling the young man behind her. As she moves through the other guests she wiggles her fingers at some, calling out, "Hi! Hi there!"

I am introduced to Karl, who is doing research related to sleeping sickness at an important institute in the city. After listing his qualifications adoringly, Inge introduces me. "He's a teacher here."

"Oh," says Karl. "What do you teach?"

"English."

"Oh," says Karl, peering around as if searching for something. "That must be very uh, interesting."

"I'm so glad we were invited here tonight," says Inge. "I really wanted Karl to see some traditional activity while he is out here at the site." Karl views the activity blankly and without comment.

"Come Karl, there's a seat over there," says Inge and drags him over to a vacant bench against the wall.

Demi's father and uncle look a little uncomfortable but more gruel is ladled out and we are soon deep into another hunting story. I glance up from time to time with growing dismay. Inge and Karl, after talking for a little while and observing the other guests, are now becoming more engrossed in each other. Inge has one hand on Karl's thigh and strokes it up and down. When next I look over he has his arm around her and one hand rests on her breast. I look around the gathering and see that this embarrasses many guests. People in this culture consider any public display of passion to be very bad manners.

I hope Inge and Karl will stop but when next I glance up they are nuzzling each other, oblivious to the effect they are having on this gathering. I stand up, shake hands with Demi's father and uncle and walk over to Karl and Inge.

"Hey, you two," I say in the jolliest voice I can muster. "What say we go drink some of that cold Heidelberg? I'm really tired of this beer porridge."

Inge looks up with a stunned expression, but a nod from Karl brings her agreement and the three of us make our departure from Amina's compound. As we follow the path to Inge's house, Karl advises me in paternal tones to go back to university and get a better degree so that I can do something more interesting.

"Now, look at this situation," he says. "Here you are teaching English in the school to a bunch of kids who probably couldn't care less. And at the same time here is Inge in the same village, digging right down into its underlife, doing important research that will probably impact on life here dramatically and make a significant academic contribution as well."

"Oh, Karl!" says Inge modestly.

"Don't undervalue your achievement," he says.

"The data you are collecting are unique, really unlike anything I've ever seen before. It's amazing!"

I remember Gibril prostrate with laughter.

"And the local people really appreciate what you are doing too," I say with conviction. "It's remarkable, the effect you are having on them."

"Of course," says Karl. "When these people are exposed to the scientific approach they inevitably see the light. I'm considering doing a field study here myself," he adds.

"I'm glad to hear it," I say. "Only today I heard that the people in Biyor are hoping for a researcher." I pause. "Perhaps *both* of you..." and I make a gesture towards the two of them as we settle ourselves on Inge's porch.

"Yes, yes," says Karl handing me a cold, green bottle from their cooler. He is interested in this information and asks whom he should contact.

"I'll find out and put you in touch with them," I say.

Afterword

It is now nearly three decades since I experienced the events that comprise these stories and nearly a decade since they were first set down in their present form. During these years the world has changed, Africa has changed and I have changed, but I still feel these stories were worth writing. I trust that, as well as some pleasure, the reader has found some value in reading them.

When I returned to Canada after spending fifteen years in West Africa, I missed it terribly. I missed the hot climate, but much more importantly, I missed the human warmth. I was also distressed by how negatively

Africa was portrayed in the media, when it was noticed at all. Wars, genocide, famine, corruption and incompetence were one face of the news. The other face of Africa was lions, giraffes, rhinos and chimpanzees, a zoologically rich setting for love affairs between Europeans. Where were the Africans I had grown to love and respect? Where was the kindness, tolerance and wisdom I experienced in Africa? Thus I determined to mine my experiences and shape some stories to bring a little balance to our picture of Africa. If the picture I've painted seems too idealized please remember that it was intended to balance a portrayal that was, and still is, far too bleak and negative.

These stories, while they are an attempt to picture a different culture, may not always be accurate in ethnographic details. I was mainly concerned to capture the spirit of the people. However well I may succeed with this, it is as an outsider, a translator rather than a genuine participant. The truest portraits of Africa will always be drawn by Africans. If this book does nothing else, I hope it will inspire readers to explore the works of authors such as Wole Soyinka, Chinua Achebe and Ken Saro-Wiwa, to mention only a few of the many fine Nigerian writers.

Villages such as those in *The Moon's Fireflies* still exist in Africa but it is a way of life that is passing. In this book I have tried to record some of the virtues of that way of life. Perhaps we can learn from them how to make our modern societies more kindly and tolerant. I hope so.

But what of Effiong and Little Etim? If I have succeeded in my storytelling, readers will be wondering about these boys. Of course they have grown up now and have children of their own, one of whom, I'm proud to say, is named after me. If through these pages you have grown to love them as I did, please remember that they are your brothers as well as mine because Africa is mother to all of us, no matter how far we may have strayed.

Benjamin Madison
Victoria, BC, Canada
December, 2009

Acknowledgements

Without the unfailing encouragement and support of my daughter, Fern Long, and her husband, Ricky Long, it is unlikely these stories would ever have made it into print. I must also thank DB, who inspired and then read the first of these stories and whose enthusiasm encouraged me to continue writing. My editor, Audrey Owen, provided stimulating support and guidance that assisted greatly in preparing the manuscript for publication. John Simmons and Corinna Zimmermann gave me good critical input as well as careful copy-editing. Special thanks to Corinna for the splendid cover art and to my grandson, Alex, for his assistance with this. Thanks also to Donna Stocker, Romi Pritchard and Garry Horne for their suggestions and support. Finally, I thank my old friend, author and editor Ron Smith, for his editorial assistance as well as for helping to make these stories more widely available..

Trained as an anthropologist, Benjamin Madison lived and worked in the West African countries of Nigeria, Togo, Ghana, Sierra Leone and The Gambia for seventeen years, generally working in Education and Development. He lived for several years as a volunteer teacher in villages such as those depicted in *The Moon's Fireflies*. "These are stories from my earliest years in Africa. I consider myself privileged to have shared the lives of villagers such as those portrayed in *The Moon's Fireflies*. Their wisdom and their warmth continue to inspire me."

Benjamin Madison now resides in Victoria and is working on a novel set in West Africa.